The New York Times

CHANGING PERSPECTIVES

Crime

T0282815

THE NEW YORK TIMES EDITORIAL STAFF

Published in 2019 by New York Times Educational Publishing
in association with The Rosen Publishing Group, Inc.
29 East 21st Street, New York, NY 10010

First Edition

The New York Times
Alex Ward: Editorial Director, Book Development
Brenda Hutchings: Senior Photo Editor/Art Buyer
Heidi Giovine: Administrative Manager
Phyllis Collazo: Photo Rights/Permissions Editor

Rosen Publishing
Greg Tucker: Creative Director
Brian Garvey: Art Director
Megan Kellerman: Managing Editor

Cataloging-in-Publication Data
Names: New York Times Company.
Title: Crime / edited by the New York Times editorial staff.
Description: New York : New York Times Educational Publishing,
2019. | Series: Changing perspectives | Includes glossary and index.
Identifiers: ISBN 9781642820133 (pbk.) | ISBN 9781642820126
(library bound) | ISBN 9781642820119 (ebook)
Subjects: LCSH: Crime—Juvenile literature. | Criminal
investigation—Juvenile literature.
Classification: LCC HV6789.C756 2019 | DDC 364.152'3—dc23

Manufactured in the United States of America

On the cover: The NYPD investigates the crime scene in 2016
where a man was shot and killed in the Bronx; Edwin J. Torres for
The New York Times.

Contents

CHAPTER 4

The 1980s and 1990s

CHAPTER 5

The 2000s and Beyond

Introduction

IS THAT A CRIME? Well, it depends. Crime is a social construct — it means what people agree it means. What constitutes a crime changes over time. And it can change depending on who is in power. Certain acts, such as rape, murder, assault and larceny, are universally thought to be criminal. But what about slavery, the exploitation of workers, extortion and prostitution? When The New York Times began reporting in 1851, these activities were not illegal. In fact, the first police forces were established in part to protect the interests of the people engaged in running such businesses. Police officers were paid to capture escaped slaves, suppress worker strikes, extract payment from small business owners for "protection" from powerful gangs and ensure that those who frequented the red-light districts paid for services rendered. In short, the police were there to protect the wealthy, educated upper classes from the "dangerous" poor, immigrants and racial minorities. Although the role of the police force has changed over time, this history has determined the ways in which we think about crime and criminals today.

Ideas about crime and criminal behavior changed significantly throughout the 20th century and into the 21st century. One way to follow these changes is to look at the criminalization of the drug cocaine. In the late 1800s, cocaine was hailed by doctors and druggists as a miraculous cure for common colds and toothaches. Immensely popular, it was added to beverages, cigarettes and beauty treatments. However, when it became clear that the drug was more harmful than helpful, heavy restrictions were placed on its manufacture and distribution. In the 1960s, cocaine re-emerged as big business on the black market. And in the 1980s, use of its high-addictive concentrated

As another driver's car is towed away in the background, a man is detained for avoiding a San Jose Police Department Sobriety and Driver's License Checkpoint in San Jose, Calif.

form, crack, had become widespread in urban black communities. Addiction-fueled property crime and gun-related homicide rates jumped. President Richard Nixon declared a "war on addiction" in 1972, and drug-related arrests became common. Prison populations exploded, and a disproportionately high number of black men were incarcerated.

This is just one example of the ways in which ideas about what is criminal have evolved. This book looks at several, including organized crime, white-collar crime, sex crimes and politically-based crimes. Some acts that were legal in the mid-19th century, such as enslavement, prostitution and selling cocaine, are criminal today. And some acts that were illegal during the early 20th century — such as selling alcohol and public homosexual behavior — are now legal. Crime changes to suit the times.

CHAPTER 1

The Late 19th Century

The first municipal police forces were established in the 1830s. Their jobs were to capture and return escaped slaves and maintain order among the people. Sometimes this meant apprehending murderers or grand larcenists, but often it meant arresting the homeless poor, the desperately hungry and the uneducated laborers drunk on alcohol sold by the barrel. Corrupt police officers were ruled by businessmen and politicians, and crime was defined as any act that ran counter to the interests of the ruling class.

Law Courts: Court of General Sessions

BY THE NEW YORK TIMES | OCT. 13, 1853

BEFORE RECORDER TILLOUS — The case of Patrick Darcy, whose trial on an indictment for manslaughter has for some days been dragging its slow length along, has terminated in a verdict of "not guilty."

COUNTERFEIT MONEY.

John Meehan was placed at the bar on an indictment charging him with passing a counterfeit Bank note for five dollars, purporting to be of the Fall River Bank of the State of Massachusetts. The District Attorney in summing up the case, told the Jury that at this moment the amount of counterfeit money in this country was absolutely equal to half the genuine notes in circulation. The Jury having found the prisoner guilty, with a recommendation to mercy on account of his previous good character, he was sentenced to five years' imprisonment.

JUVENILE CRIME.

James Hepan, a youth found guilty of stealing nine pieces of silk handkerchiefs, worth $38, the property of James S. Davies, was sent to the House of Refuge.

IMPRUDENT ROBBERY.

Thomas J. Muhony was indicted for stealing a horse and wagon, the property of Benjamin C. Leveridge. It appeared that the complainant, who is a physician residing at No. 149 East Broadway, drove, in the course of his profession, to No. 98 Chatham Street, and went in, leaving the property outside the door. On returning outside again he missed it, and it was soon afterwards found in the possession of the prisoner, at Third Avenue, near Forty-second Street. The accused could only account for his having the property in his possession by saying that he was very drunk and really did not know. The Jury, after some deliberation, found him "not guilty."

GRAND LARCENY.

Sophia Hutchinson was found guilty upon an indictment charging her with stealing a gold watch, and sentenced to three years' imprisonment.

THE HORNS OF A DILEMMA.

Francis Gallagher was placed at the bar on an indictment charging him with stealing a cow belonging to James Whalon. It appeared that the animal in question was kept in a yard, the security of whose enclosure was anything but satisfactorily established, and in some way or another found its way out thereof. The prisoner was seen by an officer leading it by the horns in Fourth Avenue, and on being questioned, was, as the police functionary said, "very scarey." He, however, subsequently stated that he found the animal, and was trying to take her home. He was, moreover, inebriated at the time. The Jury was placed on the horns of a dilemma as to whether he intended to commit a felony or not, but after retiring to deliberate, found the prisoner not guilty.

MORE COUNTERFEIT MONEY.

John Ogden found guilty on an indictment charging him with offering a counterfeit bill for $10, purporting to be on the Bank of New-York, was sentenced to five years' imprisonment.

The Court adjourned after this case.

Outrageous Rape

BY CHICAGO TRIBUNE | NOV. 21, 1856

CHICAGO TRIBUNE — Day before yesterday, a young German woman named Louisa Beurle, who lives in Rucker-street, near May-street, went to wholesale liquor store in La Salle-street to purchase a cask in which to pickle sour-krout. She was sent into the cellar, along with the porter of the store named Frederick Hollinghausen, to select such a cask as she wanted. While there, she states that Hollinghausen seized her by the throat — preventing her outcries — and, by force, accomplished his vile purposes upon her person. The girl, escaping, went directly to her friends and informed them of what had taken place. Hollinghausen was arrested, examined before Justice De Wolf, and held in $1,000 bond for trial. The accused has since been indicted by the Grand Jury.

Interesting from Kansas

BY THE NEW YORK TIMES | NOV. 22, 1856

The Law & Order Party was formed in Kansas by pro-slavery activists to target, attack and arrest people associated with the Free-State cause. The Free-State Party was a political group that fought for Kansas to join the United States as a free — non-slave — state.

Correspondence of the New-York Daily Times:

LECOMPTON, KAN., SATURDAY, NOV. 8, 1856 — After a ride of ten miles I reached this place; on my way stopped at a house on the California Road, four and a half miles from Lawrence, near the spot where the lamented Barbour fell, murdered by an officer of the Government, nearly a year ago.

The house was once the property of David Buffom, who, you may remember, was cowardly assassinated by a company of over five hundred Missourians, a few weeks since, in the presence of his Excellency Governor Geary. Near the house fell mortally wounded as brave a man as ever shouldered a rifle on the plains of Kansas; a young man, one of the earliest settlers in this Territory,

I knew him well. After being shot, he crawled to the house of a neighbor, and there with friends the brave man died, another victim to the hellish spirit of American Slavery.

During our December war he was dangerously wounded by the accidental discharge of a rifle, rendering him a cripple for life.

Mr. Buffom saw the party coming towards his house, and, anticipating their object to steal his horses, he went out and caught one of them and attempted to lead him off, but a ruffian came up and commanded him to leave or he would kill him. The cripple protested and begged, but it was of no use; others of the party were coming towards him shouting like wolves. Mr. Buffom retreated into his cornfield, followed by one of the Missourians, who shot him. He fell, the murderer came up and caught him by the throat, and commanded him to tell where his rifle was or he would kill him. Buffom said he had no rifle, and that he had been killed already by him. The cowardly assassin clutched him harder at the throat, and holding a pistol at his head said, "if he did not tell where his rifle was he would blow his brains out."

The only answer was that he had none. The ruffian left him with a curse, and saying, "that he thought he was shot enough, and would die anyhow." The dying man hobbled towards Captain Thom's, a neighbor, and he was taken in, died the next morning, saying, "he was ready and willing to die; that he was not afraid to meet death." He lingered in agony for hours, and then his spirit took its flight to another world.

The Governor and Judge Cato were present and took the testimony of the dying man.

The five hundred assassins passed on, unheeding his cries for help, and escaped. The Governor allowed them to escape without trying to bring them to justice. They were members of the "Law-and-Order Party," and privileged from arrest. Some time afterwards, however, he offered a reward for the apprehension of the cowardly assassins, and that is the end of it as far as Geary is concerned.

Slavery exists in Kansas. In this city alone there are several slaves; all of the servants at the only hotel in town are "marketable property."

The Gubernatorial mansion is presided over by one of the unfortunates, a colored woman, said to be the slave of Col. Titus. She is hired by the Governor to superintend the woman's department, and is known as "the Governor's nigger."

In Leavenworth and other towns on the Missouri river there are several slaves. Some are held by settlers on claims, many by the Shawnees, and others by the officers in the United States army. The exact number is not known.

The busiest portion of the residents of this city are the rum sellers and the marshals of the Territory. Making people drunk and arresting Free-State men is the principal business.

Nearly, if not all, of the Pro-Slavery men, have their hands in Uncle Sam's deep pocket, drawing therefrom the gold to pay them for services rendered in subduing Kansas. The number of United States Marshals and Deputies in this little "Virginia" town is not known. I am acquainted with half-a-dozen who write U. S. Marshal after their name, and I understand there are several more. One sees but few females here, "heaps of men," with nothing particular to do except hang around the three or four groceries, playing cards, drinking whisky, smoking, and denouncing Free-State men.

This is Court week, however, and there are many in from the surrounding country. With the aid of Col. Titus' company, who intend to leave as soon as their term of enlistment expires, the Pro-Slavery Party can poll about 450 votes.

At the last election Whitfield received every ballot for "Delegate to Congress."

One paper, Pro-Slavery of course, is published here, (the Lecompton Union) by Jones & Farris.

The Court was adjourned until the next regular term. The balance of the prisoners are to be examined and tried before Judge Cato, of the Second Judicial District, held at Tecumseh, and commences on Monday next.

Descent Upon the "Park Cruisers"; Thirty-Eight Arrested

BY THE NEW YORK TIMES | JUNE 13, 1857

FOR SOME TIME past the Park has been made intolerable and almost impassable by the nightly-increasing number of abandoned women, the most degraded of their class, who are there congregated. On Monday night the Sixth Ward Police arrested thirty-eight of their number and took them to the Station House. Their ages ranged from 17 to 35 years. Yesterday morning they were brought before Justice Connolly, at the First District Police Court. They had each a separate examination, and every one of them was sent to Blackwell's Island — some to the Penitentiary and some to the Workhouse — for terms varying from one to six month. Their names are as follows:

Ann McCaffrey, Ann Maria Taylor, Mary Garry, Margaret Relles, Ann Brown, Mary Keegan, Mary Ann Hudson, Emma White, Mary Ann Baker, Mary A. Murphy, Catharine Lloyd, Mary Welch, Nelly Hopkins, Maria Bresso, Ann McDermott, Mary Sullivan, Mary Ann Runyon, Sarah Fitzgerald, Mary Furrell, Ann Murphy, Ada Clark, Mary Ann McAnally, Catharine Smith, Mary Smith, Mary Ward, Margaret McGuire, Sarah Smith, Ann Moore, Catharine Wise, Matilda Foster, Ebza Burns, Mary Bernstein, Ellen Roe, Elizabeth Regan, Susan Carter, Ann Boyd.

Burglary and Heavy Robbery in New London

BY THE NEW YORK TIMES | SEPT. 23, 1857

ON FRIDAY NIGHT of last week the dry-goods store of Mr. W. P. Benjamin, of New-London, Conn., was burglariously entered, and robbed of costly silks of the value of about $4,000. Previous to the commission of the offense, the burglars provided themselves with a large tool chest, which they had stolen from a carpenter's shop near, and in this they packed their plunder. Afterwards they stole a sail boat and crossed over to Bedford, Long Island. At this point, Officer Bliss, one of the clerks in the office of Deputy Superintendent Carpenter received information that some suspicious fellows, with a large tool chest in their possession, had been seen about the place on Saturday. He, with the Sheriff of New-London, repaired to Bedford Station, and after making diligent inquiries, found the hackman who had been employed to convey the chest in question to a house in Thirty-sixth-street, near Tenth-avenue. The hackman was brought over and after pointing out the premises where he had deposited his freight, Officers Robb, Wildey and Bliss, attached to Deputy Carpenter's office, at 9 o'clock on Sunday evening surrounded the house, which they watched till daylight, when assisted by Sergeant Curry, of the Twentieth Precinct, they made a descent upon the place and there succeeded in arresting three old convicts named David Crawford, Wm. Carpenter and Thomas Downey, also Carpenter's wife or mistress, also her mother and Crawford's wife. After securing the prisoners and locking them up in the Twentieth Precinct Station, the officers searched the house where the arrests were made, and to their great delight found all the goods which had been stolen from the store of Mr. Benjamin in New London.

In addition to the property stolen from Connecticut the officers found on the premises nearly $2,500 worth of silks in the piece, costly ready-made silk and other dresses, jewelry, shawls, silver ware, cutlery, large quantities of soaps, &c., all of which property is supposed to have been stolen. On the premises jimmies, skeleton keys, nippers, several revolvers, all heavily loaded, screw-drivers, and other like implements, were found and taken in charge. The prisoners will be taken back to New-London to await their trials. Crawford has served out two terms in Sing Sing Prison; Carpenter was pardoned out of Sing Sing over a year ago by Gov. Clark, and Downey has served one term in Sing Sing, and has been out only three or four months. Crawford at the present time, as alleged, stands charged with the commission of a burglary in Sing Sing. Carpenter has wealthy relatives residing in Newburg, who repeatedly have offered to support him in affluence if he would abandon his evil course, and lead an honest life — but he preferred the excitement consequent upon a life of dissipation and crime. This is one of the most important arrests which has been made by the new police, and reflects great credit upon the officers engaged in the matter.

Heavy Sentences for Murder, Manslaughter and Assault

BY THE NEW YORK TIMES | MAY 9, 1859

Court of Oyer and Terminer. Before the Hon. Judge Davies.

THE JURY in the case of James Glass, charged with the murder of Richard Owens, have not yet agreed. They went out on Friday, at 3 P. M., and stood eleven for conviction and one for acquittal. So they remain at present. On Saturday they were twice summoned into Court, and, through their foreman, asked for instructions. It Is understood, however, that from the first moment of the trial, there was no probability that the Juror who "holds out," would agree to convict the prisoner under any circumstances. The Judge will summon them again into Court this morning at 10 o'clock,

The convicted prisoners of the term were brought into Court, on Saturday, to be sentenced. In anticipation of this scene, the Court-room was crowded with selections from each class of our worst population. There were thieves in abundance, for though no thief was to receive his reward, they have interest in the result of every crime. Prize fighters, and their colleagues, abounded, for Coburn was to be sentenced. But the friends of the brothers Glass of Higgins, and the others of the Elm Street gang, thronged every portion of the Court-room, devoted to the general public, where human beings could be packed.

On the bench, with Judge Davies were Judge Ingraham, Judge Pratt, of Syracuse, and Judge Allen, of Oswego — all belonging to the Supreme Court. Quimbo Appo was first called upon to receive sentence. He is the Chinaman who killed his landlady, Mary Fletcher, who interfered when he was quarreling with his wife, a drunken Irishwoman, who would not get his meals or in any way attend to his domestic comforts. The jury, on convicting him of the crime of murder, recommended him to mercy. Nevertheless he was sentenced by Judge Davies to be hanged on July

2, but in all likelihood the recommendation of the jury will have its affect, and his life will be spared on application to the Executive. Poor, diminutive Appo wept very much after the passing of the sentence, and looked as miserable and friendless as any human being, Chinaman or not, could look. His case attracts a great deal of sympathy.

Jean Bosquet, the man who killed the Italian boy, Martino de Santez, in Canal-street, and afterward, while confined in a ceil in the Tombs, stabbed a follow prisoner seventeen times with a fork, bending the prongs on the wretched victim's skull, was next brought to the bar for sentence. He had been indicted for murder, but owing to some doubts respecting his sanity, the District-Attorney agreed to receive his plea of Guilty of Manslaughter in the First Degree. The Judge addressed him through the interpreter, Mr. Kazinski, and sentenced him to hard labor for life in the State Prison. He was unmoved at the sentence — nothing, apparently, in the way of punishment could move him; though an allusion to the hideousness of his appearance, it is said, will throw him into a paroxysm of rage. He much nearer resembles an orangutan than a human being.

Michael Flynn, convicted of Manslaughter in the First Degree, in causing the death of Freeman Cutting, was sentenced to ten years at hard labor, in the State Prison. Cutting, as it was shown on the defence, was the assailant, but his attack on the prisoner did not by any means justify the use of a dangerous weapon.

The next prisoner, and in the estimation of a large portion of the spectators, the most important one, was John Glass, convicted of Manslaughter in the First Degree in killing Wilhelm Decker, at No. 21 Elm-street, on the 15th January. He boldly asseverated his innocence, but the Judge sentenced him to twenty years imprisonment in the State Prison with hard labor. He did not flinch when he returned to his seat, but subsequently on taking leave of his brother, who is on trial for the murder of Richard Owens, and was in Court awaiting the verdict of the jury, he burst into a violent fit of weeping and did not recover his self possession for some time.

James Higgins, convicted on the same charge, also for Manslaughter in the First Degree, was likewise sentenced to twenty years, at hard labor, in the State Prison. He took his sentence rather coolly, but presently shed a few tears, when he began to realize its importance.

The German baker, John D. Pfromer, keeper of the saloon in the Bowery, who was assaulted by Charles J. Sturgis, the noted rowdy, and who shot him dead, being in fear of his life, from Sturgis' attack, was next summoned for sentence, Mr. H. L. Clinton made an earnest appeal to the Court, on behalf of the Germans of the City, for suspension of sentence, until a bill of exceptions could be prepared. Judge Davies replied that the formality of passing sentence would not interfere with the action of the General Term on that bill of exceptions, and the District-Attorney promised to detain Pfromor in the City Prison instead of sending him to Sing Sing, till Mr. Clinton's proceedings, backed as they were by most of the leading Germans in the City, were disposed of. The sentence was four years in the State Prison. A commutation is generally expected.

Joseph Coburn — Joe, the prize-fighter — who pleaded guilty to an assault with a dangerous weapon, having been indicted for an attempt to kill Police officer Davison, was the last prisoner sentenced. Joe being very popular among the rowdy population with which the Court was well crowded, great interest was apparent when he came forward. It was a general, but delusive, opinion among his friends that he would be "let off easy." But they miscalculated, or mistook Judge Davies for a City Judge. He was sent to hard labor at the State Prison for three years. His sister, child, and a female friend, were in Court, and immediately [after] the sentence was pronounced the sister began to scream, and continued to do so, until she was removed from the Court-room. As she passed behind the Judge's chair, on her way out of the room, she shook her fist at him, and increased the volume of her scream.

The Court-room, during the passing of the sentences, was guarded by fifteen policemen, under the charge of Capt. Dowling.

Childhood and Crime

BY THE NEW YORK TIMES | MARCH 29, 1860

A DAY OR TWO SINCE, we commented upon the reply made by a convicted criminal in one of our Courts to that formal summons by which our Law, "the sum of human wisdom," after silencing a prisoner during the whole course of his trial, when his words might possibly serve the ends of justice, requests him to offer any observations that may occur to his mind upon a sentence, which he could neither shake nor change were his tongue as the tongue of an angel. The case of this man, Williams, sentenced to eight years of imprisonment, with no power in all that time to provide for the sustenance, comfort and education of four motherless children, may well arrest the attention of the most amiable of optimists upon the fearful inadequacy — to brand it with no sterner name — of our existing criminal jurisprudence, to the work which society expects it to accomplish. Our laws are supposed to be aimed not only at the punishment of crime, but at its prevention; and we make it one of the loudest of our many loud boasts over the philanthropic progress of modern times, that we have gilded the social necessity of chastisement with the divine quality of reformation, in our systems of prison discipline. Yet here we find ourselves, not only sending the criminal to pass eight years of his life, as it were, in an exhausted receiver, under an absolute vacuum of all human motives, either to amendment or newness of life, empty alike of hope and fear; but actually condemning four innocent children to that utter destitution, both material and spiritual, which is the first stage, the primary school of habitual crime. In doing this, of course, we deliberately inflict upon the community the almost moral certainty of whatever suffering and loss four young lives surrendered up, by order of the Court, to evil and that continually can prepare for themselves and us!

It is tolerably clear — is it not ? — that if all be for the best in the best of all possible worlds, the best of all possible worlds has not yet been fully

organized under the aegis of the Empire State? One of the most important elements of political economy — the economy of human character —
is still evidently susceptible of profitable cultivation by our Legislature
and our Judiciary. We achieve the penal service of the State at a quite
extravagant cost, when we are obliged to throw away four human souls
for the chance of mending one; and that protection to property is of little
value which avenges a single theft by creating a new brood of thieves.

It would be no unprofitable task to inquire how considerable the
proportion is of infant destitution for which we are indebted to the lag-
ging civilization of our criminal law, as in this case of the family of
Williams. The task is not easy of accomplishment, however, for sta-
tistical science is still in its infancy with us, and the best reports that
we have from our great disciplinary institutions are deficient in many
most important particulars.

The Twelfth Annual Report of the Inspectors of State Prisons in
New-York, transmitted to the Legislature Jan. 4, 1860, informs us that
of 153 females confined in the prison of Sing Sing, 53, or about one-
third, were spinsters. In the Auburn prison, out of 811 convicts, 431, or
considerably more than one-half, were married. In the Clinton prison
the proportion leans the other way, presenting us with 289 single persons, against 155 married or widowers. Accepting these indications,
without attempting to make them the basis of any social generaliza-
tion, and making allowance for the entire absence of information as to
the parental relations of prisoners, we may yet safely enough infer that
at least one-third of the 2,486 convicts confined in the four State Prisons alone of New-York, on the 30th of September, 1859, were heads of
families. Now if we assume that but three-fifths of this number, or five
hundred persons, represented children actually exposed to demoral-
ization or absolute destitution by their confinement, and that these
five hundred parents again represented on the average no more than
two children each, (both of these assumptions falling largely within
the probable truth of the case) we have a total of one thousand children upon whom the crimes of their parents were thus visited by our

Christian State. Utterly unequal to exposing the true gravity of the mischief as these figures are, how sadly and sternly eloquent they should be to confront our practical philanthropy and mere common sense with a social plague at once so disastrous and so absurd.

Serious inquisition into this subject will undoubtedly throw great light not only on the causes which retard the success of our efforts at reformatory prison discipline, but also on the secrets of that increasing "juvenile pauperism," the very name of which is an outrage upon our free and Christian civilization, and the existence of which is one of the most serious of our social dangers.

Ten years ago the reality and growth of this form of misery among us was suddenly revealed in the reports of the Chief of Police. These reports startled us with the knowledge that there were then, in 1848-49, nearly ten thousand children in this City who lived literally in the streets and by their wits, true Bedouins of Broadway and the Bowery.

This statement was received at first with a cry of incredulity, as it was but natural it should be; for we had thought ourselves young, and we shrank from this painful warning of approaching age. But it proved, on subsequent examination, to be too true, and, indeed, to paint the truth too lightly. Once forced upon the public conscience, the truth, of course, began to produce a certain amount of public activity. It needs little intelligence for any man to see that the question of the children is the question of our national future. The familiar financial maxim of Poor Richard has a much nobler meaning, and a much more solemn value, when we apply it to the arithmetic of human life. If we take care of the children the grown people will take care of themselves; and as the institutions of this country, above those of all the world beside, depend for their permanence and success upon the capacity of the grown people to take care of themselves, the duty of taking care of the children, is politically as well as socially the imperative dictate alike of American patriotism and of Christian humanity.

But how very far that duty still is from being adequately done, it is neither easy nor pleasant for us to set forth. Take, for example, the annual reports of such a society as the "Children's Aid," and what do we find? This society was organized in 1853, on the soundest of all possible reformatory bases in a country like our own, that of educating these savage children into human feeling, self-respect, and the power of befriending themselves. It has been administered with rare zeal and skill, proving its wisdom every year more and more clearly by its works. In the great difficulty, and perhaps impossibility, of establishing here precisely such a family system of reform-discipline as that which has been so nobly developed in France by M. De Metz, at Mettraye, and justly unwilling to risk a less thorough and Christian and well-organized attempt of the same kind, Mr. Brace, the Secretary of the Society, adopted the analogous, and in America perhaps more satisfactory plan, of first fitting these helpless estrays of the highway to know what home means, and then securing homes for them in the rich and labor-craving West. Twenty years ago, in England, Mr. Carleton Tufnell bore witness to the fact that even in crowded Britain those pauper children, who came into his hands from an individual service, were far more likely to grow into decency and to prosper, than those who were subjected to the routine of "Reformatory Mills." The experience of the Children's Aid Society has thus far more than vindicated the sagacity of its plan; and it is evident that with proper supervision, patience and discretion, no more feasible and humane system than this can readily be devised for relieving us from the fruits of this fearful social disorder, which, indeed,

"Curses deeper in its silence
than the strong man in his wrath."

Yet, what has the "Children's Aid" been able to do? During the past year it has found homes and the hopes of a new life for about eight hundred vagrant children, or considerably less than the numbers which the State, in the discharge of its criminal duties, has thrown loose during the same time upon the public! Nor is this all.

For now seven years this Society has come again and again before the community, bearing in the gone hand the terrible evidences which prove that the desperate and dangerous classes are recruiting themselves at the fountain-heads of life in free New-York, almost as rapidly as they do in the most crowded capitals of Europe; and bearing in the other hand, the list of those citizens of New-York who are sufficiently alive to the duties and the perils of their position to strengthen an enterprise which is simply the cheap police of the future. In that list, down to the present year, the wealthiest class of inhabitants of New-York — that class whose very existence is most seriously menaced by the growth under democratic institutions of a desperate and homeless population, inured from infancy to crime — has been almost entirely unrepresented.

Between this blindness of the law, and this indifference or incapacity of Property, what thoughtful man may not sometimes tremble lest the bravest efforts of the most earnest and intelligent charity should prove in the end unequal to a struggle with that rising tide of barbarism which is daily springing up in all our lanes and alleys, in the swarming passages of our tenant traps, and in the squalid caverns which honey-comb the very ground beneath our feet?

Hardships Suffered by Unionists

BY THE NEW YORK TIMES | JAN. 26, 1862

Correspondence of the Louisville Democrat:

WINCHESTER, KY., FRIDAY, JAN. 17, 1862 — To-day a poor woman, a widow, arrived here from the neighborhood of Campton, county seat of Wolfe County, having left home (once a home) to try to avoid starvation. The rebels, under Ficklin, subordinate of Humphrey Marshall, had robbed her of her all. She left home to try to find bread by begging from Union men.

Not a day passes that we do not hear of such cases. In Floyd, Wolfe, Pike, Letener, and Perry, the rebels have robbed nearly every Union family of something, and there are hundreds of families that have been plundered of their all. To the counties named may be added portions of Breathitt, Magoffin, and Morgan. Unless speedily relieved, great numbers of these people must perish. In the case of the woman mentioned, she has three sons in the Federal army. Of course she was an object of special vengeance. You and the public generally have but a poor conception of the utter and terrible destitution that prevails in the region I have named. The robbery and plundering have made every Union man's house a desolation. Every species of insult and aggravation that the malice of the robbing devils of that region could devise has been heaped upon the Union men.

It is a very grave question what is to be done for the relief of these families. Are hundreds of the women and children of the Union men of those counties to perish through hunger and cold — suffering brought on them by the robbing, murdering devils that have devastated that country? But I would call the attention of the military authorities to the fact that a large proportion of the robbers that have been prowling over that country are from some of the richer counties a little lower down. Clarke, Montgomery, Fayette, Bourbon, Nicholas, Harrison, &c., have furnished the leaders, and most of the material of the gangs that have completely despoiled that region. The secessionists of all these last named counties have, from the beginning of the rebel encampment at Prestonburgh under Williams, given the most active aid and comfort to all the robbery and spoliation that has been ruining that country. There is no longer a doubt that something must be done immediately to relieve their sufferings. Justice demands that those wealthy rebels who have in these lower counties been so active in encouraging those miscreants, shall bear the burden of supporting these destitute, starving women and children.

I trust that Gen. Buell will not, amid the multiplicity of his cares, forget the sufferings of these people, and that he will remember that the just and righteous mode of relief is an assessment on the rebels on the skirt of wealthy counties lower down, to save from the most horrid misery hundreds of families of men who have been robbed of their all, because they have been loyal to their country.

A Negro Outbreak

BY THE NEW-ORLEANS BEE | AUG. 17, 1862

NEW-ORLEANS, AUG. 5 — Around 1½ o'clock yesterday morning the Third District was the scene of one of the most desperate negro affairs which this city has yet witnessed. Shortly before that hour the Police of that District discovered coming along the levee a large band of negroes, evidently runaways, and determined to carry out their schemes at all hazards and costs. They were armed with all sorts of weapons which plantations afford, from cane bill-hooks to clubs.

When they reached about Montegue street, the police ordered them to halt, and proceeded to endeavor to arrest them. Instead of surrendering themselves, however, they immediately attacked the police in the most ferocious manner. The officers immediately called for further assistance, and were speedily reinforced, almost to the whole strength on duty in the District; but so furious were the negroes that they were in danger of being completely overcome. Their clubs and pistols were freely used, but so numerous was the gang of negroes that they were not equal to the task which had fallen on them. By this time the whole neighborhood was in a state of terrible excitement, and assistance from other quarters being absolutely necessary to save the police, a detachment of military from adjacent quarters hastened to the spot and lent their aid. It did not take long after this to convince the negroes that they were overpowered, for three of them were soon killed, a number desperately wounded, and the mass of them scattered, some running in one direction, some in another, some jumping into the river and swimming off, and so forth.

The total number of the band, it would seem, was something like a hundred and fifty; but they were not all together at the time of the police accosting them. They had run off last night from plantations down the coast. From one, that of Thomas Morgan, Esq., some thirty have run off, thirteen of whom are now in the Parish Prison, nine in the Charity Hospital and one killed.

We saw those in the Charity Hospital this morning. They are as follows:

1. Harry, 18 years of age, been on the plantation of Mr. Morgan. He is badly contused about the head and elsewhere, not so badly, however, but what he was about to be sent from the hospital to jail. He says that the gang started from the plantation on Sunday night, when the moon was about two hours' high.

2. Philip, aged 35 years, shot in the ear, and will probably die.

3. Lewis, 16 years old, severely contused about the head, but in condition to be removed from the hospital to jail.

4. Monroe, aged 20, with his skull fractured, and badly contused in various parts of the body. His condition is critical.

5. Adams, 25 years of age, heavily, hit about the shoulder, and apparently stupefied by his share in the fight. He was to be removed to jail.

6. Hossy, aged 32, badly beaten about the head with clubs; kept in the hospital.

7. Braxton, aged about 50 years, born (not like the preceding ones on the plantation) in Virginia, severely hit on the back of the head, and with contusions elsewhere. He was to be removed to jail.

8. Joe, aged about 60, like the foregoing, from Virginia, shot in the upper part of the thigh, and severely contused with club blows.

9. Johnson, aged about 50, born on the plantation, shot in the thigh; severe cut over the eye; badly beaten over the head.

After the mastery had been obtained over the gang, they were taken to the Third District Police Station; but Mr. Holland, the Clerk, seeing the condition of those above mentioned, considerately sent them to the Charity Hospital.

Beside the three killed and the nine wounded negroes above noticed, there are others also more or less hurt.

Four of the Police officers, we regret to learn, are pretty badly injured.

We presume the Coroner will hold an inquest on the bodies of the three killed negroes, when we expect further and perhaps more accurate details.

The affair has created great excitement throughout the city, especially in the lower districts; but this is nothing in comparison to what exists in the country below. Apprehensions of the gravest character are felt on all the plantations, and measures for protection against the dreaded evils are being most anxiously canvassed.

The Confession of Constance Kent

BY THE NEW YORK TIMES | SEPT. 12, 1865

DR. BUCKNIL, of Rugby, the medical gentleman who visited Constance Kent to give an opinion on the subject or her sanity, has published, at her particular desire, a confession which she made to him of her crime. On the night of the murder she undressed herself and went to bed, because she expected that her sisters would visit her room. She lay awake watching until she thought that the household were all asleep, and soon after midnight she left her bedroom and went down stairs, and opened the drawing-room door and window shutters. She then went up into the nursery, took the child from his bed, and carried him down stairs through the drawing-room. Having the child in one arm, she raised the drawing-room window with the other hand, went round the house and into the closet, lighted a candle which she had secreted there, and placed it on the seat of the closet, the child being wrapped in the blanket from his cot and still sleeping; and while the child was in this position she inflicted the wound in the throat with a razor of her father's which she had procured a few days previously. She says that she thought the blood would never come, and that the child was not killed, and she thrust the razor into its left side, and put the body with the blanket round it into the vault. She went back into her bedroom, examined her dress, and found only two spots of blood on it. These she washed out in the basin, and threw the water, which was but little discolored, into the foot-pan. She took another of her night-dresses and got into bed. In the morning her night-dress had become dry where it had been washed, and she folded it up and put it into the drawer. Her three night-dresses were examined by Mr. Foley, the Police Superintendent, and she believes also by Mr. Parsons, the medical attendant of the family. She thought the blood stains had been effectually washed out, but on holding the dress up to the light, a day or two afterward, she found the stains were still visible. She therefore secreted the dress, moving it from place to place, and she eventually burnt it in her own bedroom, and put the ashes or tinder into the kitchen grate. As regards the motive of the crime, says Dr. Bucknil, it seems that although she entertained at one time a great regard for the present Mrs. Kent, yet if a remark was at any time made which, in her opinion, was disparaging to any member of the first family, she treasured it up and determined to avenge it. She had no ill-will against the little boy, except as one of the children. Dr. Bucknil adds, "She told me when the nursemaid was accused, she had fully made up her mind to confess if the nurse had been convicted, and that she had felt herself under the influence of the devil before she committed the murder; but that she did not believe, and had not believed, that the devil had more to do with her crime than he had with any other wicked action. She had not said her prayers for a year before the murder, and not afterward, until she came to reside in Brighton. She said that the circumstance which revived religious feelings in her mind was thinking about receiving the sacrament when confirmed." The doctor does not believe Constance Kent is insane, but he thinks from her peculiar temperament that solitary confinement would be very likely to make her so.

The Ring Again; Another Batch of Indictments Against Tweed & Co.

BY THE NEW YORK TIMES | MARCH 10, 1871

Tammany Hall was a Democratic Party–based political organization in New York City from the 1780s through the 1960s. Supportive of immigrant-owned businesses, it was dedicated to expediting the economic growth of its constituency. Leaders of Tammany Hall had enormous political control, and some, such as William "Boss" Tweed, used that to accrue great wealth and power.

A TIMES REPORTER met a gentleman with whom he has a passing social acquaintance, and who has been long noted for his staunch support of Tammany Hall, and besides, draws a regular revenue from the City Government. The gentleman to whom the reader will be introduced was found at a time and place not important, and the conversation that is to be recorded commenced in a spirit of badinage, at the apparently absorbing interest which the adherent of Tammany seemed to take in a copy of the Daily Times, which he was perusing.

REPORTER (smiling) — Are you a subscriber for the Times, Mr. ——?

The gentleman who, in virtue of his influence in the tribe of Tammany, and for convenience shall be designated as Little Chief — his real name being withheld for obvious reasons — replied that he read it as often as any other paper.

REPORTER — I thought you were too warm an adherent of Messrs. Tweed, Sweeny and Connolly to pay for a paper that places them before the public in such an unenviable light.

LITTLE CHIEF — Well, perhaps it is caused by a desire to read what Republicans think of them, but with all of its growling, I think it makes small headway against Bill Tweed, Sweeny, and Connolly.

REPORTER — Well, that remains to be seen, Mr. —; the old saw says, in substance, that a drop of water, falling constantly in the same spot, will wear a stone and newspaper iteration will tell if it is only kept up long enough, especially if it is a constant detail of facts.

LITTLE CHIEF — Well, there is some truth in that, and I'll be hanged if these fellows who talk about the jobs in the Times ain't posted. I know enough to know they are from the way they talk, and I'll bet old Tweed and the rest of them wince when they read the record of their high crimes and misdemeanors, he concluded, laughingly.

REPORTER — As you seem to be satisfied of the rascality of the Ring, how would you like to tell me as a Times reporter, what you know about their dark doings?

LITTLE CHIEF (surprised) — I didn't know you were a newspaper man; however, it is no matter, but I'll tell you, Sir, that you Republicans haven't half as much cause to growl as we have on our side. Why Tweed, Sweeny and Connelly rule the party with an iron hand; they do just what they please with it. If you want to get a nomination for office, you must get their approval; if you want an appointment, you must have their sanction. The Board of Aldermen are now rendered a nonentity, and "Boss" Tweed is their dictator. A man may be ever so popular in his own ward or district; if he has incurred the displeasure of any of these three men he has the greatest difficulty to obtain a nomination. The big political balls and receptions gotten up during the Winter were to show the local strength of the men in whose honor they were given; but it does but little good unless they are willing to become the creatures of the Ring.

REPORTER — You speak of Tweed, Sweeny, and Connolly particularly, and leave out Mayor Hall and a number of others thought to be equal partners.

LITTLE CHIEF — Tweed, Sweeny and Connolly are the rulers. The rest are only their creatures. Tweed, Sweeny and Connolly control the finances, and that is the secret of their power. They buy the Press; they buy the Legislature; they buy men whom it would be supposed were not to be bought; and Tweed spends the stolen public money so liberally, and offers such enormous bribes — if he thinks it necessary to carry a point — that but few men can withstand his temptations. He buys men in your party, as you know, and that is where he is beginning to make himself weak; he is not keeping before him the Democratic principle "take care of your friends," and in his bribery of Republicans, he is neglecting those of his own party who have the strongest claims upon Tammany Hall; and that is what is going to fetch him in the long run.

REPORTER — Are not Tweed, Sweeny and Connolly very popular in their districts?

LITTLE CHIEF — Tweed is popular enough in the Seventh Ward, and he ought to be among the ignorant, as he threw away $30,000 to $50,000 among them, which they couldn't see was filched from them, in common with every one burdened with taxation in this City. Sweeny could not get elected to the Assembly if he should run on his merits, and Connolly is exceedingly unpopular in the party.

REPORTER — I shall begin to regard you as a sympathizer with the Young Democracy, Mr. —.

LITTLE CHIEF — No, Sir. I have always worked and voted with Tammany, and always will; and if either of the three men was to run for Governor in the next election, I'd vote for him if he was the nominee of the Tammany Democracy. Still, I would like to see the whole gang out of power. They are going too far, want too much, and have too much power.

REPORTER — Well now, Mr. —, will you tell me what you know about the doings of the Ring?

LITTLE CHIEF — Well, I don't know that I can tell you anything newer than what has been published; but I'll tell you all I can think of at present.

REPORTER — Well, a repetition of their rascalities may serve to give them thorough ventilation.

LITTLE CHIEF — There are the Park Commissioners, who are practically: Peter B. Sweeny, Henry Hilton and Thomas C. Fields. Look at the power they have got. Why they can spend as much money as they please, and how is the public to know how much they do spend?

REPORTER — They certainly have extraordinary power; as I understand it they have the power to alter the face of the whole City above Fourteenth-street if they so will it.

LITTLE CHIEF — Yes, they are empowered to construct, maintain and have the care and custody of all parks and public places in the City of New-York, as well as the public drives and boulevards, and are also empowered to lay out and construct all streets above Fourteenth-street. That is nearly the language contained in the act creating them, and does not include many other powers conferred upon them in the act. Why, Sir, the construction of the eastern boulevards, to run along the east side, and to form a junction with the western boulevards, will be millions of dollars in their pockets.

REPORTER — And so you think that the gentlemen of the Park Commission, under the guise of public improvements, are only intent on improving their personal fortunes, and hide their robberies of the City Treasury with park shrubbery?

LITTLE CHIEF — That's true. I tell you, Sir, they know how to feather their own nests as well as do the sparrows. The Commission either derive a revenue in that way or give their friends an opportunity to grow rich at the public expense. They don't care as long as they can benefit by it, how much it costs the City. Washington Parade Ground might have had whatever alterations made that were rendered necessary by the widening of Laurens-street, at much less expense than it promises to cost at present. Why, Sir, I estimate that $150,000 has been spent already, and one-third of the work is not yet done that is mapped out, to complete the alterations begun.

REPORTER — The Park Commissioners are authorized to call on the Controller to issue bonds for the expenses of their Department at any time, if I remember rightly?

LITTLE CHIEF — Yes; and you can bet that they call often enough; and the Controller knows better than anybody else the reason why.

REPORTER — These bonds issued by the Controller bear seven per cent interest, do they not?

LITTLE CHIEF — Yes; and they are very good property. They are issued in the anticipation of the payment of taxes, and for adjusted claims, and are redeemable every year. They are taken up by Savings

Banks — the Bowery Savings Bank buys a good many of them — and capitalists like John J. Astor, Henry Rhinelander, and others, invest heavily in them. These bonds are not always redeemed at the time of their expiration, but are allowed to run on, and the holders are, of course, well enough satisfied, as the investment is perfectly safe, and they reap a good rate of interest.

REPORTER — The City might be saved a good deal of money on their debt if more stock were issued running for a longer time and at a lower rate of interest.

LITTLE CHIEF — You mean, like the regular City stocks and securities, that run for twenty and thirty years at six per cent interest? That would do, you see; the public could then make a shrewd estimate of the City's debt, as these stocks are a matter of public record. The City Revenue Bonds can be sold privately, and nobody but the seller and buyer need know who holds them unless they are offered for sale on the street. If the Controller wants a million of dollars in a month, he issues these Revenue Bonds, in anticipation of money to be raised by taxation, and goes out among those who are eager to get possession of them, and borrows money without the necessity of asking authority from an inquisitive body of Common Councilmen.

REPORTER — Why, it is equal to manufacturing greenbacks at will.

LITTLE CHIEF — Over three million dollars' worth of these bonds have been issued for the payment of claims, adjusted by the Controller, under the power given him by the legislative act of 1868, abolishing the Board of Audit, a former creation of the Legislature, and transferring their powers to the Controller. The Controller's power for the adjustment of claims still exists, but the Mayor and Commissioners of Public Works now share the labor and emoluments with him.

REPORTER — Watson used to be the particular confidant of the Controller, was he not?

LITTLE CHIEF — Yes, Watson made his first big money by acting as a go-between with Connolly and persons who had claims to adjust. Any one who wanted to see Connolly had first to "see" Watson — that is to say, they had to "come down with the stamps."

REPORTER — I suppose there is no doubt in your mind that Watson was the catspaw of the Ring in the Broadway widening job?

LITTLE CHIEF — None in the least. The exposure of that job is one of the most telling blows that has been dealt at the Ring. There is one job, however, that I have never seen much publicity given to, in connection with the Fiske pavement. In the act passed by the Legislature of 1869, for a tax levy, a clause was inserted to provide for the appropriation of $250,000, or so much thereof as may be necessary, for converting the City Hall Park into an open plaza, and paving Fifth-avenue and other streets with concrete pavement. In the final engrossing of the tax levy, after its passage, the word "thereof" was by some mysterious cause omitted, which, of course, increased the amount granted to indefinite limit. There was such an outcry, however, by the Press and public against the pavement, which proved to be so worthless that it had to be stripped from Fifth-avenue, that much to the loss of the Ring and the benefit of the public, the streets of New-York were saved from being totally plastered with the Fiske concrete pavement.

REPORTER — And Mr. —, you are satisfied, though a Tammany Democrat, to have this conversation published?

LITTLE CHIEF — Yes, if it will do anything toward the downfall of the Ring. I am glad to offer it as my mite for the good of the party; but of course as my position, and the power which the Ring have at present to crush me politically, depends upon my name being kept secret, I hope you will not mention it.

Applicants Ruled by Politics

BY THE NEW YORK TIMES | DEC. 22, 1894

Police and political corruption were so widespread that an investigation by
the Lexow Commission on Criminal and Political Corruption — also called the
Lexow Committee — was started in 1894. Named for the committee's chairman, State Senator Clarence Lexow, the committee collected more than 10,000
pages of testimony describing extortion, bribery and the abuse of power.

WHEN CAPT. SCHMITTBERGER came into the courtroom, he took a seat near
the counsel's table, next to the one occupied by Police Justice Voorhis.

The Police Justice and the indicted Police Captain shook hands.
Schmittberger appeared to be unwilling to talk, but Justice Voorhis
kept looking at him in a curious way, as if trying to fathom the work-
ings of his mind.

As soon as Mr. Goff entered he called Capt. Schmittberger to the
stand. The Captain had already been sworn, and Mr. Goff started in
upon his examination without delay.

"You are called here, Capt. Schmittberger," said Mr. Goff, "as a
witness for the State of New-York to testify about matters connected
with the Police Department of the city. In taking the oath do you
recognize its obligations?"

"Yes, I do," said the Captain in a low voice.

"You know that your oath is binding on your conscience, do you?"

"Yes."

"And you have come here to tell the truth, the whole truth, and
nothing but the truth, without a reward or a promise of a reward having been made to you?"

"I have."

"Now, the law extends certain privileges to you," went on Mr. Goff.
"Outside of these privileges are you prepared to tell everything without hope of any reward?"

"I am."

Mr. Goff asked Chairman Lexow to state to the witness the attitude of the committee toward him. Chairman Lexow said:

"We have proved certain corruptions to exist in the Police Department of this city, but we are here to prove that a system of corruption exists and not that any individual corruption exists. If any witness comes here to aid us in the work of discovering this system, we consider it out of obligation and duty as Senators and individual citizens to throw about him every protection that we can. If you decide to tell unreservedly all you know about the corruptions which exist, we shall see to it that all the immunities shall be thrown about you. We believe that an individual case of corruption is insignificant compared with the whole question involved."

Capt. Schmittberger said he joined the force Jan. 28, 1874, when he was twenty-two years old. He was married at that time, and had previously been a confectioner.

"Did you pay anything for your appointment as a patrolman?" asked Mr. Goff.

"No."

"The practice had not been commenced at that time?"

"No."

"The civil service system was not in existence then, either, was it?"

"It was not."

Capt. Schmittgerger said he was first connected with the old Twenty-ninth Precinct, now called the Tenderloin, where he was a patrolman for three years. He said he had become well acquainted with the methods of the police, and with the wickedness which was prevalent in that district.

FAVORITES AMONG PATROLMAN.

"Were there any favorites among the patrolmen at that time?" asked Mr. Goff.

A. "Oh, yes; there are always favorites."

Q. "They got considerations of one kind and another?"

A. "Yes."

Q. What were these?

A. Well, being excused from duty, or being given particular assignments. There are lively posts and dead posts. A policeman likes to get on a lively post, where there are people to be seen, and where he can get a sandwich and a cup of coffee. He does not like to go where it is desolate.

Q. Who are these assignments made by?

A. Usually by the Sergeant, sometimes by the Captain.

Q. Are patrolman ever dissatisfied with the assignments they receive?

A. They are.

Q. What effect does this favoritism have on the force?

A. Well, a Sergeant might be more interested in one man than another. There are other reasons. I don't know that I could give any others, though.

Q. We have been told that politics had something to do with the making of these assignments?

A. It has a great deal to do with it.

Q. What is the effect of this?

A. It is decidedly detrimental.

Q. Under such circumstances, then, the Sergeant becomes the mouthpiece of the politician, does he?

A. Yes.

Q. The politician goes to the Sergeant to get him to extend favors to his political friends?

A. Yes, that's the way of it.

Q. The Sergeant must realize that the politician has some influence over him if he does that?

A. Undoubtedly.

Q. With whom?

A. With his superior officers.

Q. And this might result in his removal if he disobeyed the politicians?

A. Yes.

Q. When he applies for promotion, does he not rely upon politics to help him?

A. Yes, he relies more on his political "pull" than on his record as a policeman.

Q. We have been informed that the Sergeants have also been influenced by other considerations than political ones, such as the financial consideration, in making the assignments of the patrolmen to certain posts, or in excusing them from duty?

A. I do not know of such a practice. I have never known them to give anything more than cigars. Such a case never came under my personal consideration; but I have heard of such cases.

DO NOT MAKE GOOD POLICEMEN.

"How does the class of men appointed on the police force during the last ten years, from 1884 to 1894, compare with those appointed during the years from 1874 to 1884?" asked Mr. Goff.

A. Those who were appointed during the previous ten years are better patrolmen.

Q. Why?

A. Well, the men who have been appointed during the last ten years do not appear to be so strong and able, notwithstanding the civil service examination. They don't seem to "catch on" to their duties. They are better politicians than policemen.

Q. We have heard that applicants for positions on the police force have to pay for their appointments; is that so?

A. It is a matter of common rumor.

Q. Would that tend to the deterioration of the force?

A. It would.

Q. Can you give us any information on that subject?

A. I cannot tell you anything about payment for appointments on the force, but I can about payment for promotions.

Q. We have heard that "go-betweens" got the money paid by policemen?

A. Yes, I have heard of that. Their names are very well known.

Q. Can you give any of their names?

A. Charley Grant, Commissioner McClave's secretary.

Capt. Schmittberger said he had read about a man named Kelly or O'Kelly, and that he had heard of a tailor named Myers, near the Metropole Hotel, as a "go-between," but had never known of Alderman Parks, except through the newspapers.

Q. So far as the discipline of the force is considered, what is your experience with men who have paid for their appointments as to their reliability and good service?

A. They make poor policemen. They feel as if when they had paid for their appointment they had certain rights which the others didn't have.

Q. Are they more disposed to do clubbing than older?

A. Yes. They have more independence, and don't seem to care. They don't obey orders as well as the older men.

Q. Suppose these men break the laws and are brought to trial, what is their attitude?

A. They feel that they have a right to protection because they have paid for their appointment. They depend more on their political "pull" than on their defense.

A Remedy for Many Ills. The Great Demand Springing Up for Cocaine.

BY THE NEW YORK TIMES | SEPT. 2, 1885

RECENT PUBLICATIONS on the subject of cocaine and the various thera-peutic uses to which it can be put have caused a widespread demand for this valuable drug. This increased demand for cocaine is a source of marked satisfaction among all the druggists because, like every-thing else which is new and valuable, it commands a large price and insures a handsome profit. The new uses to which cocaine has been applied with success in New-York include hay fever, catarrh, and tooth-ache, and it is now being experimented with in cases of seasickness.

The present call for cocaine comes mostly from sufferers from hay fever, whose attention was directed to its beneficial results by the pub-lication in The Times recently of an article from the London Lancet. The article printed by the Lancet epitomizes a review on the subject of using cocaine in nasal disorders by Dr. F. H. Bosworth, of New-York, and contained in the Medical Record of Nov. 15,1884. Briefly, Dr. Bosworth claims to have tested cocaine in 40 cases of Autum-nal hay fever, nasal polypus, and catarrh, with marked success. The great advantages are that in cases where the use of a knife or snare is necessary, the anaesthetic effects of cocaine relieve pain and also cause a severe contraction of the membranes, driving away blood and reflecting the smallest blotch, so that a surgeon may easily perceive and remove it. Scarcely any blood follows this sort of operation when cocaine is used, whereas by the old plan of operation profuse bleeding always follows.

The doctors say cocaine is bound to be a blessing for that source of horrible annoyance so easy to obtain and so hard to get rid of — a cold in the head. Hereafter public speakers, singers, and actors will not be permitted to plead "cold in the head" as an excuse for disappointing their audiences, nor will the man who uses final "b" for final "m" be tolerated. All will be given to understand that cocaine will cure the worst cold in the head ever heard of. If a man exclaims that he has toothache as only a man who has toothache can exclaim, somebody at his elbow will shout, "Rub cocaine on It." Or if a child has the earache cotton and laudanum will be forgotten as its mother asks for the cocaine jar. It is the contemplation of these little matters that makes the druggists happy, for they are assured beyond doubt of the absolute excellence of cocaine treatment in cases such as indicated.

At the office of the Medical Record. No. 56 Lafayette-place yesterday, Business Manager G. P. Castle said: "The medical world first heard of cocaine as an anaesthetic through a correspondent sent by us to the Medical Congress at Copenhagen in 1883. Here Dr. Koller read a paper on the subject which we secured. His theories were taken up and not only all that he and our own Dr. Bosworth have declared possible has been proved, but there is a universal medical belief that many blessings will yet result from experimenting with cocaine."

CHAPTER 2

The Early 20th Century

Crime during the early 20th century was perpetrated largely by syndicates organized and run by the dominant political parties of the time. Prohibition allowed these syndicates to develop sophisticated bootlegging operations to satisfy the enormous black-market desire for alcohol, all with the assistance of a corrupt police force. Extreme poverty during the Great Depression led people to commit smaller crimes, such as petty theft. Even men dressing as women was an arrestable offense.

Becker Wore Women's Clothes and Whiskers

BY THE NEW YORK TIMES | AUG. 30, 1904

NEW ROCHELLE, AUG. 29 — Christian Becker, who for twenty years has masqueraded as a woman, and who gives an address in West Fiftieth Street, New York, was arrested here last night. He was tastefully arrayed in a black picture hat, a pink shirtwaist, and a tight-fitting skirt. His shoes were high-heeled, and his carriage was strictly in accordance with the "straight front" decree.

He had just introduced himself as "Emma" Becker, and was enacting the role of hostess at an ice cream table when Police Sergeant Kelly took charge of him. This morning, when brought before Judge Van Auken, still in his feminine outfit, he admitted that the role of a woman was no new thing for him.

"I have been passing myself off as a woman for twenty years," he confessed. "I am a cook by profession and find it easier to get work as a woman than as a man. I have never been caught before. I worked for President Roosevelt's family once."

"Four months for you, Emma-Christian," said Judge Van Auken. "You ought to be ashamed of yourself."

The unveiling of Christian was largely due to the clever work of Miss Elizabeth Taylor, who was, until recently, a detective in a New York department store. Miss Taylor was enjoying an evening stroll on North Avenue last evening, when Christian accosted her,

"Can you tell me where an ice cream saloon is?" he asked. "I'm that tired and flustered that something cold would be fine."

"Certainly, Madame," said the ex-detective, and then she hesitated. There was something wrong about the stranger. Miss Taylor couldn't tell just what. In consequence, when the stranger asked Miss Taylor if she would not join in the ice cream, she consented. As they were about to enter the place Miss Taylor saw Sergt. Kelly, and signalled him to stand by.

Miss Taylor seated herself at a table with the stranger, and noticed that the veil worn by the masquerader was of much heavier texture than the season demanded. Sergt. Kelly was at a table near by.

The ice cream was served, and Miss Taylor noticed that the stranger did not lift the overhanging veil, but passed the refreshments in under it. Sergt. Kelly had meanwhile sized up the impostor and moved closer.

"My name is Mrs. Emma Becker," began Christian, "and I live at —" but the Sergeant gave no opportunity to finish the sentence.

"I don't know what your name is," he interjected, as he lifted the veil, but it isn't Emma. You've have a pretty close shave, but you've got a heavier beard than I have."

For a moment Becker tried to brazen it out, but once in the cell he told the story of his deception. "I haven't been a woman all the time," he said. "When I could get a job as a chef I was a man."

While serving four months in the Kings County Penitentiary women's clothes will be denied him.

Gangsters Again Engaged in a Murderous War

BY THE NEW YORK TIMES | JUNE 9, 1912

A SLIMY CHAPTER of New York life has been brought to public attention by the gang feud that broke out during the early hours of last Monday morning in the back room of a Chinatown saloon, and that has since been brazenly continued with revolvers and dynamite bombs in various parts of the city.

The quiet, law-abiding, stay-at-home citizen may think that the existence of these gangs does not concern him, that their feuds, gunfights, and murders are simply the more or less interesting outcroppings of the underworld life that exists in every big city.

But here is a fact that should concern even the most quiet, law-abiding, stay-at-home citizen: These vicious gangs are important — sometimes decisive — cogs in our electoral machine. In exchange for their strong-arm work at primaries and on Election Day there are politicians who will see that these "gorillas" have practical immunity in their life of graft and violence during all the other days of the year.

When Monk Eastman, one of the most notorious gangsters that this city ever produced, went down to Long Branch and "did up" James McMahon, the coachman of David Lamar, he was defended by Thomas F. Grady, State Senator of New York.

If the Paul Kelly Association had kept as a club totem a mammoth gun it would have been notched from muzzle to butt. Kelly himself, however, has "only done a nine-months' bit on the island" for assaulting a drunken man in Elizabeth Street. There was always some unseen but powerful influence that reached out and saved Kelly from more serious charges. It may be added casually that back of the bar in "Little Naples," the dive that Kelly ran in Great Jones Street in which Bill Harrington was shot to death, there hung a portrait of Big Tim Sullivan.

Louis Poggi, known in gangland as "Louis the Lump," was sent to Elmira for "at least a year" for killing "Kid Twist" and "Cyclone Lewis" at Coney Island in May, 1908. Recently, when he was arrested in this city for carrying a revolver, he was bailed out by a downtown Tammany Alderman, and promptly jumped the $4,000 cash bail.

This spectacle of a thug hurdling a four-thousand-dollar bankroll to liberty gives a true idea of the lush days in which the New York gangster now lives.

Times were not so good when Monk Eastman punched, blackjacked, and shot his way to the leadership of his gang. Monk began his activities as a bouncer in New Irving Hall, the successor of the old Walla-Walla Hall. Gradually his influence spread and he collected about him a nucleus of followers which later expanded into the gang which bore his name. But even in the heyday of his power he undertook the job of beating up Lamar's coachman. He had two assistants with him in this little affair. After kicking and stabbing the coachman, they jumped into a cab and disappeared.

"Doing up" a man for cash — amount dependent on the prominence of the victim and the seriousness of the injury to be inflicted — is still one of the business assets of the gangster. But nowadays, the leader of a big gang would scorn such work — unless the price was very high. The bruising he leaves to his henchmen, while he himself runs a gambling joint, a saloon with dance hall appurtenances, or engages in the equally lucrative work of holding up those that supply these kinds of pleasures to New Yorkers.

The gangster is out first, last, and all the time for money, for graft. It is the one thing that he fights over. On the surface it may occasionally seem that he fights for "honor," but it must be remembered that the moment he loses his reputation as a "bad man" his only business asset has been discounted.

That's why he never "squeals." "I ain't no squealer," is his proud boast, even when he lays at the point of death from the revolver, knife, black-jack or brass knuckles of a rival. But as a matter of fact he is entitled to little pride in the boast. He knows that if he dies having "squealed" will do him no good. If he lives, having "squealed" will put him out of business as a bad man: it will show that he can't stand on his own two feet and take care of himself, but must call on the "bulls" — the gangsters' name for police — to square his accounts with his enemies. Keeping their mouths shut when officers or the law are about is simply a matter of good business.

Writers who wish to throw the glamor of romance over the doings of these thugs tell us that some of their feuds begin over women. In the present imbroglio one Wanda Murphy, a Chinatown blonde, has been dragged from her tenement obscurity to supply the romantic hue.

But no gangster ever fought over a woman as a normal man fights over a woman. To a gangster a woman is simply a commercial proposition that can bring him in so much revenue nightly. It may be remembered that the "cadets" that made the old "red light district" what it was were practically all members of east side gangs.

No, Wanda Murphy, the Chinatown blonde, was not the cause of the present excitement among the "guerrillas." Commissioner Doughterty was right when he said that the gangs are fighting over "business matters."

"Business matters" in gangland is the polite term for any means of annexing easy money, or graft. The present pistol-punctuated feud is a patent illustration of this. In the underworld the victim is as much of a law-breaker as his parasite. The gangster is the protector and the bully of the crook.

In the old days the divekeeper was his own strong-arm man. He was usually an ex-prize fighter or a thug, and was well able to keep his own order. But there has come a change over the Bowery, the lower east side, and let us add, over certain parts of Broadway, for the gang ster, like all business, has followed the uptown movement.

The profits of the low saloon have brought into the business many men who have more coin than broad-shouldered dynamics. The business of these men is to get a customer to spend all that he has in his pocket. Needless to say, when the patron has done this he is oftentimes

"Gun Men" of Two Rival Bands of the Underworld Using Bullet, Knife, and Dynamite on Each Other "For Business Reasons."

Clockwise from top left: Spanish Louis, "Monk" Eastman, Kid Griffo, "Rough House" Hogan and Paul Kelly.

a nuisance and a disturber of traffic. Then the saloonkeeper's one wish is to get rid of him. This is where the gangster, who usually has a pal or two with him, comes in handy. The alcoholically enthused customer quickly finds himself in a little discussion, which terminated rapidly with himself on the sidewalk regarding the closed doors of his erstwhile place of entertainment.

Another field of the gangster's activities is in performing somewhat similar strong-arm offices for poolroom and gambling house proprietors. Being without the law himself, the gambling house proprietor has no redress when his protector turns parasite. The gangster is always out for money. When he cannot get enough for services rendered, he can usually keep his pockets lined by blackmail. The stuss and crap games of the east side pay tribute gladly to be left alone.

But there is another field which is even more lucrative. The hold-up game is one of the most profitable business ventures of the gangster.

Clockwise from top left: "Yakey Yake" Brady, "Eat-Em-Up Jack" McManus, Jack Zelig and "Humpty" Jackson.

It was one of Kid Twist's favorite commercial operations. He used to walk into a stuss or crap joint and say:

"I want fifty dollars. What, you're not going to cough up? I'll shoot up your —— place." When he got his fifty, he would say: "I'll see you again in about a month."

Naturally the proprietor of these joints decided that protection would be cheaper than continual dribbles of graft. With the knowledge loose in the neighborhood that Kid Twist or Paul Kelly was a "friend" of the place the lesser lights of graft kept hands off.

But it followed that the fact that a member, usually the leader, of a gang had assumed protection of a joint that had formerly been the pasturage of the member of another gang, bred bad blood and made "business reasons" for trouble among the gangs.

It is just such a bone that the gangs are snarling over to-day. The stay-at-home citizen may not realize that Chinatown is a highly popular place for those who do not wear queues or manipulate a flat-iron over shirt bosoms for a living. Every sight-seer that comes to New York, and their number is legion, must include in the things he or she does a slumming trip to Chinatown.

This neighborhood has two joints which are the chief rivals for stammers' cash, one owned by Jimmy Kelly and one owned by Jack Sirocco.

For some reason the former place has had the greater part of the very profitable sight-seeing patronage, so much so that Sirocco was stirred to go upon the war path. You see "business reasons" were once more stirring gangland. One night last Winter he waited with a number of his henchmen at Mulberry Bend for Kelly and his men. The moment the latter aggregation turned the Bend the Sirocco outfit opened fire. The Kellyites promptly returned the compliment. As a result of the fusillade — as so often happens in these interchanges of revolver shots between warring gangs — an innocent passer-by was hit. Louis Poggi, one of the Kelly adherents, was the only person arrested.

With this gun-fighter in jail Kelly realized that in order to hold his place of vantage as gatherer-in-chief of the Chinatown slummers' money it was necessary for him to get a new artilleryman.

He enrobed under his banner "Big Jack" Selig, who had already notched his gun and qualified in all ways as an east side gangster.

The raid on the Chinatown saloon, the subsequent shooting of Selig as he left the Criminal-Court Building, the bombs that were exploded in the lower Fourth Avenue neighborhood, and various other strategic moves of the gangsters are all matters that have so recently been in print that it is not necessary to recount them here.

In all these doings the Kelly and the Sirocco factions are no more than maintaining the traditions of New York gangland.

One need only jump back a few years in his memory to recall when the Monk Eastmans and the Paul Kellys were at war.

An historic battle was fought on Rivington Street, under the Allen Street elevated structure. Fifty men in all, including several policemen, stood behind iron pillars and blazed away at one another, while panic prevailed in the stores and tenements of the neighborhood. Several men were wounded and a number arrested, Eastman among them. But Monk was acquitted. In those days he was always acquitted, although his record at that time included some twenty arrests.

Meanwhile certain Powers That Were brought it home to both Eastman and Kelly that these shooting matches were productive of more harm than good.

Peace was fairly well maintained until one of the Kellys, by the name of Ford, manhandled an Eastman gangster named Hurst. Monk Eastman's men said that Ford must die. The Powers That Were urged the two gang leaders to meet, and both of them being "practical business" men, agreed to the arrangement.

The meeting took place at Chrystie and Grand Streets. The two gangsters eyed each other, taking mental stock, shook hands with grins that passed for smiles, and then, with big cigars in their mouths — neither drank — sat down to discuss ways and means for the prevention of an outbreak between their followers. A prizefight between the two was eventually agreed upon, and it was decided in a barn in the Bronx, with the two factions adequately armed, on either side of the ring. Several outbreaks were imminent in the course of the bout, and the leadership of the two chieftains was never tested so thoroughly. To their credit, be it said, that every one arrived in the Bowery with pistols still loaded and knives unstained. Thereafter peace prevailed between the two factions.

Before leaving Monk Eastman, lest any one underrate the casualties of these gang fights, a little incident be recounted. Three years ago this September a man walked into the Harlem Hospital and asked to be operated on immediately. He had some internal trouble which was causing him agony.

When the man was finally put on the operating table the surgeons were astounded to see the scars of four stab wounds, several bullet wounds, and a wound under the right arm evidently made by some blunt instrument. When he came out of the anaesthetic and was resting comfortably in bed, one of the surgeons asked him about his numerous scars.

"Oh, I've been in war," replied the man.

"The Spanish war?" suggested the surgeon.

"No; half a dozen wars down on the east side. I'm Monk Eastman."

This man's old rival, Paul Kelly, is perhaps the most successful and the most influential gangster in New York history. Like many another gangster who has taken an Irish name, Kelly was of Italian parentage. His real name is Paulo Antonio Vaccarelli. He went to the public schools of New York and for a time held a job as book-keeper in an Italian bank.

Even as a boy he was fond of boxing, and was the best fighter in his school. One night he entered one of the bouts held by an "athletic club" of the lower east side. It was an informal affair, and as he entered the ring the announcer asked him what his name was. As, most of the spectators were Irish, he realized that if he gave his name as Vaccarelli sympathy would not be with him. So, on the spur of the moment, he said, "My name's Kelly." He won the fight and he stuck to the name of Kelly.

He entered other fights, and as he won most of them he quit book-keeping and went into pugilism exclusively, fighting many of the best featherweights of the country. Then he became a manager of fighters, running as a side issue a crap game. About this time he was taken up by one of the leading Italian gamblers, known in downtown Little Italy as the "main guy."

Meanwhile he had gathered about him a following of young men, and he became a power from the Battery to Fourteenth Street. In those days he had many able gun men with him. Of these only a few need be mentioned. There was Phil Casey, shot through the head in a little row in the Cafe Maryland; Joe Morrell, killed a few months ago in Second Avenue; Spanish Louis, who was shot in Fourteenth Street; and Kid Twist, who went to his last account in Coney Island.

It was during this rise to power and affluence that Kelly acquired The Brighton, a notorious dive on Great Jones Street. Late one night in November of 1905, a policeman passing this place noticed that the lights were out and the place seemed to be deserted. The bluecoat began an investigation. He peered through the windows and cautiously tried one of the doors. It yielded under pressure. The policeman entered the barroom, and under the sickly pale light that sputtered from a single gas jet he made out the legs of a man, and following these up he found that the man's head way wedged under the bar rail. It was the body of Bill Harrington, and the proprietor and the gang had disappeared.

Biff Ellison, who was allied by friendship and other interests with the Five Points gang, in which Jack Sirocco and Jimmy Kelly were captain and lieutenant at the time, was arrested. Here, by the way, we find our friends of the present gang feud, Jack Sirocco and Jimmy Kelly, acting together. At the present moment they are at pistol points. It simply goes to show that loyalty lies where the graft is, and also how involved are gang politics.

At the trial, which occurred four years later, it was shown that Biff Ellison went up to the Brighton for the single purpose of "starting something" that was to end in the murder of Paul Kelly. Sirocco, three nights before the killing of Harrington, had been shot down on the threshold of The Brighton. He got a nasty, but not dangerous, wound. The Paul Kellys alleged that he got what he came to give or cause to be given. They also volunteered the information that Sirocco and Jimmy Kelly planned revenge and that Biff Ellison volunteered to carry the vendetta right up to the vest buttons of Paul Kelly and finish him for all time as a leader of gun men and the wielders of sling-shots.

The agile Kelly, familiar with the sight of gun muzzles, was quick enough to side step, and Harrington, the innocent by-stander, was killed. Ellison got a long term in the penitentiary on the charge of man-slaughter for this shooting.

After the slaying of Harrington, Kelly went to Harlem, where he stayed in hiding until the police found and arrested him. He was later released by the Coroner on $1,000 bail. Only a few nights before the Harrington murder Jack Rotta had been killed in the same joint, and there was some belief that the second death had come as the result of the first tragedy. However, the death of Harrington put an end to "Little Naples," and Kelly left downtown gangland. It was at this time that Jack Sirocco and Chick Tricker got the Five Points Gang in good working shape.

Kelly, after his release by the Coroner, opened a real estate office uptown and affiliated himself with a political club run by Nick Hayes, former Sheriff of this county. It was only a short time later that he appeared in the new role of a walking delegate for the Scow Trimmers' Union.

To some this may seem like a fall of life, but it must be remembered that scow-trimming is a profitable job, and that with the men who do the actual work, properly organized or intimidated, much good might result to the person holding the reins of the Scow Trimmers' Union.

As has been said, when the Harrington trial came on Kelly disappeared, to promptly reappear the day after the trial was over. Kelly now runs a gambling house in the heart of the Broadway district. It has been raided time and again by Commissioner Waldo's strong-arm squad, but within a half hour after each raid it has been doing business at the same old stand. Croupiers, dealers, and doormen have been arrested, but though Kelly himself has usually been present, the detectives have not been able to "get anything on him."

He and Kid Griffo, another east side gangster, usually dine in one of the well-known Broadway hotels. A man who is familiar with New York and its inhabitants called the attention of the manager of this hotel to these two patrons:

"Do you know who those men are?" he asked. "They are two east side thugs, and I wouldn't allow them in if I were you."

"You bet I know who they are. I won't say anything to them. I don't want to start anything around here."

The man who was familiar with New York thought that the manager of this Broadway hotel was weak-kneed until he read of the gang shooting at the Criminal Courts Building on last Monday morning. Then he decided that perhaps after all he did not know as much about New York as he had thought.

Bootleggers Seize Agent as Hijacker

BY THE NEW YORK TIMES | AUG. 9, 1924

CHARLES DIXON, a negro member of Prohibition Director Merrick's staff, reported yesterday he had been kidnapped by bootleggers during a raid in Newark early yesterday. Thinking him a hijacker, Dixon said, the band took him down the Passaic River in a rum runner but released him later unharmed.

Dixon and William Harvey, another negro dry agent, acting on instructions from Director Merrick, went to a river wharf in Newark at the foot of Chapel Street early yesterday. Information had been received that a large delivery of liquor was expected. The two agents discovered a rum boat emerging from the shadows alongside the dock where three motor trucks were already waiting. The truck crews sprang aboard the craft and made quick work of transferring the cases to the lorries, and the boat then cast off and drifted into the stream.

Dixon and Harvey took stations at the land end of the pier, barring the way with drawn revolvers when the three loaded trucks attempted to leave, according to Dixon's report.

"Hijackers!" shouted the driver of the first truck.

An automobile suddenly appeared behind the two dry agents, containing, police said, William Lillian of Newark. Lillian took sides with the truck men, according to the official version, which further asserted that when Harvey said he and Dixon were prohibition enforcement agents Lillian refused to take his word for it. Lillian and Harvey grappled, and a general fight started as the others came to Lillian's assistance from the trucks.

"Get 'em on the boat'." one cried and Dixon was rushed back along the wharf. He was put into a small boat and taken to the rum runner in midstream.

Word of the trouble reached the Third Precinct Police Station, and reserves rushed to the wharf. They found Lillian and Harvey still engaged in a violent rough and tumble, they said, but Dixon was nowhere to be found, and the rum boat had disappeared.

Lillian and Harvey were both taken to the police station where Harvey showed his credentials and was released. Lillian was held by United States Commissioner George R. Sommer in $1,000 bail for the Federal Grand Jury on a charge of violating the Volstead act. Later he was also arraigned before Acting Judge Guthrie in the Criminal Court on a charge of felonious assault, and was held in $500 bail for the Essex County Grand Jury.

A general alarm was sent out from Newark Police Headquarters for the missing Dixon as well as for the trucks and the rum runner. Some time later one of the trucks, still loaded with the alleged contraband, police said, was found abandoned in front of 104 Ferguson Street, Newark. Its gasoline tank was empty.

While the hue and cry was at its height, Agent Harvey was called to the telephone in the office of Detective Captain Frank Brex to find Dixon at the other end. Dixon reported himself safe and sound, having been released by the rivermen at the Lister Company dock, well down the Passaic River.

About the same hour as the New Jersey raid the Sandy Hook Coast Guard patrol sighted a craft stealing along the Coney Island shore, off Nelson's Point. Captain Loren Tilton, in a small speedboat, accompanied by M. W. Rasmussen, new Superintendent of the Fifth Coast Guard District at Asbury Park, overtook the boat after a sharp chase. Three men aboard surrendered and offered no resistance when their 250-case cargo was confiscated.

The prize was brought to the Battery last night, where it was identified as a 21-knot speedboat, the "108-60." It was a cabin cruiser about 35 feet in length and valued at $9,000. It was equipped with two 225-horsepower Dolphin motors, but was making only about 12 knots an hour when captured, its gunwales being almost awash with its heavy load. The liquor was unloaded for transfer to the United States Army base Brooklyn. The prisoners said they were Charles Alien of

530 Fifty-third Street, Brooklyn; John Shannon of 25 South Street, and John Coffman of 25 Myrtle Avenue, Newark.

Earlier in the day 650 cases of liquor from the schooner Pacific, which was seized at Greenport, L. I., Tuesday morning, were unloaded at the Battery. The vessel was turned over to the customs marine patrol. It was understood that the two prisoners captured on the Pacific by Agent James Ziegel were released on bail in Greenport, the amount of bail not being given.

Three boxes marked "German leaping toys" started leaking noticeably after brief handling in the offices of the American Railway Express Company at 316 Amsterdam Avenue yesterday. Prohibition Agent William Vogt was called in to investigate, and he reported that the "toys" were non-refillable bottles of Scotch whisky. The shipment had been sent from a Broadway address in the "roaring Forties" and was consigned to a woman in Cape May, N. J.

Director Merrick, in reviewing the work of the past six months said yesterday that in that period his men had captured more than $500,000 worth of liquor, and more than $250,000 in automobiles and boats. He specially cited the work of the Long Island Sound patrol, comprising six prohibition agents, who had seized 9,000 cases, 22 boats and 200 automobiles and trucks, and had raided at least ten prominent road-houses and some twenty-five smaller speakeasies.

Fire which police attributed to the explosion of a fifty-gallon still they said they found at 282 East 152d Street, the Bronx, caused minor damage to a two-story frame building there and resulted in the arrest of Felix Grande, 41 years old, who occupied the building. Patrolman Talty of the Morrisania Station charged him with violation of the Volstead act after he said he found three other stills, two barrels of mash and a quantity of denatured alcohol on the premises.

Liquor Still Flows into Boston

BY THE NEW YORK TIMES | MAY 9, 1925

BOSTON, MASS., MAY 8 — Despite the visible tightening of the warfare against rum-runners, liquor is still being landed in this section, though in lessening quantity, it was admitted today by Federal officers. These are quoted as saying that the shore in this particular section is now the only markedly vulnerable section along the New England coast.

TERRORIZING SWAMPSCOTT WOMEN.

Bootleggers and their friends evidently are trying to terrorize Mrs. Gertrude L. Hanna and Mrs. Grace Seward into silence or flight. These are the women whose testimony resulted in the bringing of charges against Police Chief William L. Quinn, alleging that he aided rum-runners in landing their stuff.

The chief hearing began yesterday before the town's Board of Selectmen, and both women have appeared as witnesses. As a result, they have received no less than fifty telephone calls and nearly a score of anonymous letters. All are in the same vein. "Keep your mouth shut or you'll be sorry," is the wording of many.

Mrs. Hanna and Mrs. Seward, according to their testimony, were present in the home of Harry Brown, 38 Melvin Avenue, when "hush money" was paid to Chief Quinn. Mrs. Hanna, it is alleged, stood but two feet away when Quinn received $1,200.

Mrs. Hanna says that men she does not know have called at her home and informed her it would be a good idea to keep away from the hearing and not say any more about the Chief of Police. She says she intends to do her duty.

The hearing before the Selectmen involves the Chief's dismissal only. It is likely that other charges will be brought.

Quintet Raids Drake Hotel

BY THE NEW YORK TIMES | JULY 30, 1925

CHICAGO, JULY 29 — Following a sensational hold-up of the Drake Hotel in mid-afternoon in which between $5,000 and $10,000 was stolen and one employee killed and another seriously wounded, the boulevard system of Chicago's fashionable North Side was the stage today for a battle with five bandits which resulted in the death of two of the robbers and the capture of one other.

Two of the bandits made their escape, and none of the money had been recovered up to a late hour.

The hold-up took place at 3:30. Then came, in the attempted flight of the gunmen, more than an hour of guerrilla warfare over North Side boulevards and streets. For a time Lake Shore Drive, Lincoln Park and Sheridan Road were battlefields for moving actions, in which pistols kept up an intermittent rattle. Robbers leaped from seized cars and seized others. Policemen commandeered passing motors and gave chase.

When the affair was over it was found that of five bandits who projected and carried out the robbery two were dead and three in custody; a hotel clerk had been killed; three persons were wounded; two women had been injured; and as a finality one of the captured bandits confessed fully, relating all the details of the mid-afternoon murder party.

The casualties in the hold-up and escape were as follows:

DEAD.

Frank Radkey, a clerk at the Drake Hotel.

Ted Court, a bandit known as "Texas," formerly of New York. He had been in Chicago only a short time.

Neils Nelson, another bandit, formerly employed in the Drake Hotel and the Belmont Hotel as a waiter.

WOUNDED.

Carl Anderson, cashier of the Drake Hotel, shot through abdomen.

Reported in grave condition.

Charles Fiorino, a Yellow cab chauffeur, struck on the head by Nelson in his flight. Not serious.

Policeman Clarence Dalof of the Lincoln Park force, shot through the hand.

The captured men, who confessed, gave the names of Jack Holmes, Joe Todd and Slim Holmes. Court was declared by himself to be a full-blooded Cherokee Indian. His home was in Sweetwater, Texas. The New York addresses which Holmes gave was 375 West 125th Street.

POLICE DEPARTMENT MOBILIZES.

The excitement caused by the raid was communicated over the city with the speed of lightning. Within a half hour after the occurrence State's Attorney Crowe had surrounded himself with a staff of assistants and had taken the field to assume direct control of the preparation of evidence. Chief of Police Collins, aided by Deputy Zimmer and Captain Shoemaker, chief of detectives, and a squad of other officials, took charge of the investigation.

Before sunset the State's Attorney's office swarmed with men, women and children gathered from over a district more than six miles long and two miles in width, all of whom had been witnesses to a few or many of the incidents in the robbery, the flight or the running warfare that spelled the end of the escapade.

Tonight State's Attorney Crowe and Chief Collins were emphatic in praise of the Lincoln Park policeman, who acted with notable celerity in all phases of the affair. Both bandits were slain by Lincoln Park policemen and the first capture was made by them.

The names of the five bandits were given out by the police and Mr. Crowe tonight. One of those killed was Neils Nelson, a former waiter. He had been employed in the Drake Hotel and also in the Belmont Hotel. The other slain bandit was variously known as Ted Court and Texas.

CHOSE A SWARMING SCENE FOR ROBBERY.

To picture the robbery it is necessary to visualize the importance of the Drake Hotel in point of location and in the number, prominence and wealth of its guests. There is a steady rumble of all manner of automobile traffic past its doors almost day and night. The wide corridors in the first and second floors are the scenes of daily promenades. The lobbies are always populated with noted persons from over the world, and to add to the dangers invited by the prospective bandit the house fairly swarms with employees of all calibres, from managers to a host of minor help.

And yet into the very heart of this building, which covers nearly a square block in extent, the five robbers penetrated today at a time when the hotel was busiest, when automobiles were rolling past all three sides in a steady stream, when porters and bellboys were running about and when the corners outside, were guarded by at least four policemen.

The Drake Hotel is bounded by Walton Place on the south, Michigan Avenue on the west and Lake Shore Drive on the north. Every side exposed to the widest observation.

It is regarded as obvious to the police, from the identification of the body of Neils Nelson, one of the robbers, that the robbery was planned on the inside. Nelson had been a waiter in the Drake Hotel, and more recently had been employed as a waiter in the Belmont Hotel.

Nelson and his three companions entered from the north or Lake Shore Drive side. Policemen were on traffic duty on corners and others were on call near by.

This northwest entrance led the robbers into a broad lobby, following which lobby they proceeded into the basement barber's shop and up a flight of stairs into the lobby known as the Avenue of Palms. At the north of this they took the stairs to a long mezzanine promenade, leading into a narrower corridor, to the front of the hotel, into a portion partitioned into various offices, cages and vaults devoted to the hotel's administration.

CLERKS IN A PANIC.

In the main clerical office were a number of clerks and hotel officials. In the northwest corner of this room is the cashier's cage. Here stood Carl Anderson, the cashier. Two of the bandits entered this main room. Three others remained in the corridor outside. Of the two who entered the room, one went straight to Anderson's cage and covered him with a shotgun.

Meanwhile the young women and men, all clerks, seated at their desks, started a mild panic. The fifth robber, later identified as Texas Ted Court, obviously drunk, was swaggering about the room with a pistol and shotgun. These he brandished about while he seasoned his remarks with profanity and threats of dire consequences if his orders were not instantly obeyed.

"Get up," he ordered. "We're from Texas. Stick up your hands."

Harry Ewer, a bookkeeper, readily complied. Seated near him were Miss Stella Boyle and Irene Bergendahl, assistant to Miss Boyle. Then, too, there were Miss Edvia Lovegreen, secretary to the auditor; W. H. Vallette, the controller, and George Barr, a clerk.

All these now were standing with hands upraised and awaiting the next command of the robber. Pointing his pistol toward a door which led into the office of Mr. Vallette, he directed all to march into the room. This they did.

Then they were marched into the office of F. B. C. Morris, promotional manager. Next, at the command of the robber, who by this time seemed to relish his mastery of the situation, they executed a right face and marched into the office of John B. Drake and that of Tracy Drake. This having been done to the satisfaction of the bandit, he ordered a retreat. The clerks and auditors executed an about-face and all marched back through the string of offices into the clerical room from which they had originally emerged.

Texas seemed more and more struck by the success of his manoeuvering. He immediately ordered a repetition of the whole manoeuvre. And again the thoroughly frightened clerks marched through the rooms again, and again returned to the clerks' room.

But while the marching and countermarching seemed to be the idle concern of a drunken bandit, there appears to have been a plan concerned in it. For when the whole office force was first marched out the robber who had all this time been standing at the back of Anderson's cage spoke quietly to Cashier Anderson and accompanied his speech with a gesture of his gun.

"Give me that cash and keep your mouth shut."

Anderson, still unaware of the hubbub that had preceded this unexpected visitation, smiled as if he suspected a joke. "What can I do for you?" he said.

GUNS TO RIGHT AND LEFT.

The robber did not answer. Instead he waved his pistol negligently as if to say "take a look behind you."

Anderson did look behind him. There were two wickets in the wall, one to the right and one to the left. At each of the wickets stood a bandit with a sawed-off shotgun leveled at his head.

By this time the humor of the situation had disappeared and Anderson threw open his cash box and invited the robbers to help themselves. The quiet man who had done the talking entered the cage and began scooping up the money. He was reaching for some small silver coins when one of his companions outside the wicket called to him:

"Forget that small change; grab the big bills."

And this he did, stuffing some $10,000, according to a later count, into a small black bag.

While this was going forward, Texas, drunken and swaggering, who was conducting the counter-marches, had robbed Ewer of a watch and Barr of a watch. Miss Bergendahl managed to slip her diamond ring into her mouth and thus saved it. Texas spied a small gold ring on her finger, studied it a moment and, then decided he did not want it.

Then he marched his charges back into the clerical room for the last time. And as he did so he met an unexpected repulse. One of the girls, being the last in line, slammed the door in the robber's face. For a moment he tried the knob, then kicked upon the panel and finally backed off and fired through it. The girls, however, were prepared for this. They sped swiftly into an open vault in the rear of the room and cowered in a corner. Texas now ran through another door and came out in the corridor through which he and his companions had first entered. As he did so, he ran into Miss Vera Blancher, secretary to Mr. Drake. The collision was so forcible that Miss Blancher was precipitated down the marble stairs, in which fall she sustained severe hurts. But hastily gathering herself up, she ran to a telephone and notified James McMurdy, house defective, whose office, singularly enough, is just around the corner and not more than twenty feet from the scene of the occurrences going forward.

Texas, having bumped into Miss Blancher, was thrown out of his course end through the door which led back into the room filled with clerks and attaches. Made savage by the door slammed in his face, he swung his pistol and fired point blank at Frank Radkey a clerk, who was sitting quietly by waiting for the end of the drama. Radkey was shot through the abdomen. He slid to the floor without a word. He was removed to Henrotine Hospital, where he died at 7:30 o'clock.

Texas trotted out into the corridor again and this time approached the door to McMurdy's office.

"Oh, McMurdy," he called.

McMurdy had been warned of the presence of the robbers and cautiously opened his office door. He held a large pistol in each hand. Before him he saw Texas, staring, cursing, and he fired.

A bullet struck Texas in the shoulder, passed through and buried itself in the wall behind.

FLIGHT BEGINS.

Then the robbers' flight began. Three ran headlong past McMurdy's door west in the narrow corridor which leads to the north and south mezzanine.

They reached the mezzanine and ran north. Texas wounded and bleeding, wrought up the rear.

By this time an ominous quiet was invading the scene of the robbery.

Radkey lay on the floor fatally wounded. The girls and other clerks were cowering in the vault. And Anderson with John Sedlack, the paymaster, who had been forced back into another and smaller vault in the rear of the cashier's cage, were awaiting a chance to emerge.

William R. Hicks, Superintendent of Service, had, in the meantime, been notified of something wrong and he came up in time to find McMurdy emerging from his office with a gun in either hand. Hicks also was armed. Together they ran down the corridor taken by the robbers. The trail followed a sprinkling of blood in the carpet.

The promenaders in the Avenue of Palms scattered for safety as they caught sight of five robbers, all armed, one (Nelson) carrying a black bag and one from whose wound a flow of blood was making carmine the marble stairs.

Another abrupt turn to the basement stairs up which they had come and still another after they gained the basement and the robbers were on the verge of safety in the open. Together they burst through the great swinging doors and made east along Lake Shore Drive.

The flight of the robbers was made severally. While three were running down the corridors, two others were flying elsewhere. The one called Joe Todd, or Holmes, ran in the rear of the cashier's cage and bounded down a flight of stairs leading to the main kitchen. On his way down he met Allen Bashara, an assistant steward.

To him he called "stick 'em up" and began firing wildly without hitting any one. Bashara tumbled down the stairs. The next to meet the bandit was Gus Garika, a coffee boy. Garika threw up his hands and was thrust into a pantry by the robber.

POLICE ARE SUMMONED.

By this time Ernest Hagkwist, kitchen clerk, ran into the street and called Lincoln Park Policemen Clarence Dalof and John Kelly. As the two policemen entered Holmes flew at them in a drunken rage. In the scuffle Dalof was shot through the hand.

Pots and pans and dishes went clattering over the floor as the policemen struggled with the bandit and finally, perceiving the impossibility of subduing him peaceably, Kelly rapped him on the head with his club. Todd dropped. It was two hours in the Chicago Avenue police station before he could be restored to consciousness.

The other sector of the fighting was now developing round Texas and Nelson and two other robbers, who were now concentrating their forces and making for an automobile parked east of the hotel and headed east in Lake Shore Drive. Texas ran aimlessly east and attempted to clamber into a motor parked in front of the hotel, evidently mistaking this machine for the bandit car he sought.

At this point two other policemen arrived. They were Patrick Hannigan and Walter Noonan of the Lincoln Park force. Hannigan and Noonan ran round opposite sides of the car which Texas was endeavoring to enter. As the bandit saw he was cornered he renewed his pistol fire, but aimlessly and without harm. Hannigan drew a careful aim and fired. Texas dropped. He was removed to Henrotin Hospital, where he died.

The remaining bandits now gained their car. This was a light green machine. They instantly got under way and drove east around the outer drive and then back west into Michigan Avenue, and then with a burst of speed gained Lake Shore Drive North. It was now the chase settled down to a running battle with dozens of cars and police, and with the result that Nelson was shot and killed at 1451 Foster Avenue in a fight with more Lincoln Park police.

ROBBERS' CAR WRECKED.

At Center Street the robbers' green car crashed into a car containing some women who fled when it became apparent that gunplay was imminent.

"I was driving there," said Walter Wendland, "when I saw this Cadillac hit the touring car. Three men jumped out of the green car.

Two came out of the front seat and one man leaped out of the rear. This last man had a black bag."

The man with the black bag was Nelson. An auto was coming south. Nelson brandished his gun, stopped the car and forced the occupants to quit it. He then tried to start this machine, without success. Nelson evaded his pursuers, ran out into the drive and piled into a Yellow cab driven by Charles Fiorino. In the cab was Miss Maisie Larson. The bandit forced her to the floor of the car, ruthlessly tramped on her, shoved his gun against Fiorino's neck and ordered him to "drive like hell." Fiorino drove through the park, north on Sheridan Road.

Policeman Wingren set out in pursuit on the running board of a commandeered car. Every policeman he passed he hailed, and the officers commandeered cars and joined in the pursuit.

West on Irving Park Boulevard they went, the Yellow cab still flying in the lead, and with Nelson shooting at intervals from the window. Policeman Kiefer in a taxicab driven by Earl Neil, pulled close up and the officer and the bandit exchanged shots. They turned north on Southport Avenue, swung into Clark Street.

A dozen officers in as many cars were in pursuit, and literally scores of civilian drivers had joined the procession. Just north of Winona Avenue Fiorino, the Yellow cab driver ran his cab into a south-bound street car. He jumped out, his arms in the air crying to the bandit for mercy. But the bandit, with policemen pouring down on him, was more interested in his own safety.

LAST STAND IN AN ALLEY.

Leaving his empty gun and a bottle of moonshine behind Miss Larson on the floor of the cab, he ran east on Winona Avenue to the alley. There he ran north and plunged down the steps of 1454 Foster Avenue. On his heels were policemen Broecken and Kiefer, both of the Lincoln Park force. Broecker grappled the bandit. Neither officer knew that Nelson had abandoned his gun. Kiefer fired the shots that ended the career of the waiter who had turned bad man.

Kiefer has held the revolver championship of the Lincoln Park force for four years. His name stands at the top of the list of eligibles for promotion to a sergeantcy.

Nelson was supposed to have had in his possession when he commandeered a Yellow cab the proceeds of the robbery, estimated at around $10,000, but no trace of it had been found at a late hour tonight. It is supposed it was left in the wrecked cab and appropriated by some bystander.

Several women, taken to the State's Attorney's office during the night, were found to have little or no information relating to the men with whom they had been associated.

One of these, Mrs. Ruth Nelson, wife of the bandit leader, declared she had never known of her husband's bandit activities. Another held for a short time was Margaret McPherson, a waitress employed at Ohio and Clark Streets. She gave the police this note written by Court: "Dear Margette: Can't see you tomorrow as I have an important engagement to keep. Will tell you about it Friday at 4 P. M. Tex Ted Court."

The important engagement proved to be his death at the hands of a Lincoln Park policeman in front of the Lake Shore Drive Hotel, just east of the Drake.

Association Aids Crusade on Crime

BY THE NEW YORK TIMES | AUG. 2, 1925

THE ALLIED BUSINESS MEN'S PROTECTIVE ASSOCIATION, INC., with headquarters at 291 Broadway, unanimously adopted a resolution yesterday endorsing the National Crime Commission movement and anti-crime crusade proposed last week at a meeting of prominent men in the offices of Elbert H. Gary, head of the United States Steel Corporation.

Members of the association, discussing the crime situation, agreed with the recent statement of Mark O. Prentiss, one of the leaders in the movement that it is "terrifying beyond all expression." Although it was admitted business had suffered heavy losses through the brazen activities of the modern criminal, with his ready pistol and his purring automobile ready for the "getaway," this fact was not more stressed in the discussion than was the loss of life through crimes of violence and the danger to life in hold-ups and crimes of that character.

Members of the Allied Business Men's Protective Association, it was said, have sought to have officials of the organization take some step to show that they are ready, individually and as an organized body, to support the anti-crime movement among business men and officials, and to give it their active cooperation.

BUSINESS MEN'S RESOLUTION.

The resolution of endorsement reads:

> "Resolved. That the Allied Business Men's Protective Association, Inc., tenders its hearty cooperation to the newly organized movement to establish a National Crime Commission, which has for its motive a movement to combat the terrific evils existing in the way of crimes committed by murderous assaults, and in the scheming and manipulation of those engaged in the perpetration of crime, so notoriously known to exist in this country, whereby it may be ascertained just how far the police, the prosecuting officials, the judiciary, and the parole boards of the country may be found to be at fault in encouraging and aiding those enemies of

society to the end that the criminal laws may be remodeled and their sphere of usefulness enlarged and encouraged by a stricter enforcement and by obtaining cooperation and quicker action among the punitive agencies throughout the entire country."

Officials of the association expressed the opinion that while the existing Criminal Code might be made far more effective against criminals, amendments and alterations would materially strengthen it and should be drawn and put into effect.

Communications received by the leaders of the National Crime Commission movement indicate that interest in it is very general and is by no means confined to this community or State. Letters from individuals in both the South and West indicate that crime in those sections is now recognized as a menace to be met by organized business, by the citizenship of the country whose lives and property are both endangered.

At the next meeting, to be arranged for in detail tomorrow by Mr. Prentiss, Assemblyman F. Trubee Davison of Glen Cove. L. I. and one or two others, probably including Franklin D. Roosevelt and Judge Gary, there will, it is said, be prominent persons from other cities and States, as the movement is essentially national.

CRUSADE TO BE NATION-WIDE.

Mr. Prentiss pointed out that the National Crime Commission is not to be a body that will go after any one set of officials, or any man or body of men of one city, but will investigate crime and methods of combating it in many sections of the United States.

Where it is found that anti-crime methods are least effective, such a community will be appraised of that fact and will be informed also of more effective methods which may have been put in operation in other sections. The movement, Mr. Prentiss said, may result in something akin to a unification of crime-fighting methods, and certainly will bring into much greater and closer cooperation the punitive agencies throughout the country.

Although prohibition has been mentioned in connection with the movement, its leaders are anxious to have it understood that the National Crime Commission will not concern itself with the Volstead act and its enforcement. The only connection prohibition has with the movement is of that variety outlined Friday by Judge Alfred J. Talley, who said the prohibition law, in his opinion, was "responsible for all our lawlessness and disregard for constituted authority."

In view of discussions that have developed ever since the first meeting regarding where to place the blame for existing crime conditions, it is said the first step of the Crime Commission will be to look carefully into the phase of the situation. Already it has been charged that punitive agencies have displayed jealousy of each other and have thereby lost a degree of their effectiveness.

If Governor Smith puts through his proposal for a State Crime Commission, with power of subpoena, such a commission, leaders of the national movement say, will probably place New York out in front as leading the nation-wide anti-crime crusade, and dissemination of such information as may be obtained by the State Commission will, it is believed, prove a great help to other crime-ridden States and communities.

Anti-Crime Body to Organize Today

BY THE NEW YORK TIMES | AUG. 12, 1925

THE NATIONAL CRIME COMMISSION expects to complete organization today at the biggest meeting yet held in the interest of the movement. It will begin to function at once and in the open, according to Mark O. Prentiss, authorized spokesman, who said the closed-door sessions had been necessary in the formative stage because "so many big men were being discussed and placed where they belong in the crusade of organized business against organized crime."

In its search for information that will aid in decreasing crime in this country the commission would have "hearings," Mr. Prentiss said, to which officials of the punitive agencies would be "invited." Asked if the commission would have power to compel the appearance of any official before it, Mr. Prentiss replied that there would be no need of compulsion, for the various officials undoubtedly would volunteer to give all the information they had. He added that public sentiment would be too strong for any official to refuse to appear before the anti-crime body.

Just what punitive agency would first be asked for furnish information relative to its methods of operation Mr. Prentiss would not say, but he intimated this activity will begin very soon. The commission does not propose to attack any one, Mr. Prentiss said, but it is understood that dissatisfaction over the failure of law enforcement was the primary cause of the movement.

OFFICERS TO BE NAMED TODAY.

Twenty-three leading citizens of this and other cities, some outside of New York State, have notified Mr. Prentiss that they will attend the meeting today in the offices of Elbert H. Gary, head of the United States Steel Corporation, at 71 Broadway. George W. Wickersham will preside as temporary Chairman. Mr. Wickersham is also Chairman of the Organization Committee, which will meet at noon to complete its slate of officers and executive committee men to be presented to the larger meeting at 2:30 P.M.

The Crime Commission expects soon to establish international connections, and it will thus become an active part of a world movement to abate criminality and particularly crimes of violence.

"It is inspiring," said Mr. Prentiss, "to see that forces all over the world are concerned with this problem of crime. The International Prison Congress in London has the same objective we have to make the whole world a better and safer place for law-abiding persons to live in. We are not prepared yet, however, to discuss the merits of the recommendations made at the London conference."

TALLEY ASSAILS ONE SUGGESTION.

Judge Alfred Talley of General Sessions declared some of the recommendations made by congress in London to be "plain foolishness."

"The recommendation that Judges receive compulsory education in psychology, sociology, &c., is just plain foolishness," he said. Our need is for Judges who know the law and who exercise their judicial functions with a view to the best possible protection of the community they are supposed to serve; men who have the courage to face unpleasant duties without flinching.

"What we need also is prisons that are prisons — not country clubs, radio parlors and recreation centres."

Poverty and Crime.

LETTER | THE NEW YORK TIMES | AUG. 23, 1925

IF THE National Crime Commission confines its interests to mere palliatives and such superficial poultices as your correspondents do in today's Times, it will waste its efforts.

The fundamental cause of crime is poverty. Only so far as such commissions point out a remedy for undeserved poverty are they helpful.

Today's crimes of violence are due mainly to our taking millions of men and teaching them to disregard the sacredness of life and property rights. Until they forget what war taught them, we must endure these war-taught evils.

Such laws as the Sullivan law, which deprives law-abiding citizens of weapons to resist hold-ups and burglaries, help extend the saturnalia of crime by insuring protection to criminals from their victims.

WILL ATKINSON, CAPON SPRINGS, W.VA., AUG., 12, 1925

30 Taken in Bronx Raid

BY THE NEW YORK TIMES | JAN. 4, 1930

THIRTY MEN were arrested for disorderly conduct yesterday in a raid on the Bronx Independent Democracy, Inc., on the second floor of 370 East 140th Street, the Bronx. Detectives also entered an alleged speakeasy on the first floor, which has no connection with the club, and arrested Joseph Miller, 38 years old, of 915 Brook Avenue, charged with possession of liquor. Edward O'Brien, 30 years old, of 420 East 155th Street, was arrested on a bookmaking charge in the club quarters.

The raid was made by detectives under Lieutenant Frank Wood of Chief Inspector O'Brien's staff on complaints received from neighbors. The detectives allege a card game was in progress and bets on horse races were being received in the club rooms. More than fifty bottles of liquor were seized on the first floor and in the basement. According to the police, the club is a social organization without any political affiliations. The club was not known at Bronx Democratic headquarters.

Champagne Seized in Hoboken Dry Raid

BY THE NEW YORK TIMES | DEC. 31, 1930

DEPARTMENT OF JUSTICE agents from New York raided a restaurant at 74 Hudson Street, Hoboken, last night, seized 1,000 cases of champagne, liquors and fine wines and arrested the two alleged proprietors on charges of manufacturing illegal beverages and conspiring to violate the prohibition law.

This was one of fifteen raids in and around New York staged yesterday by dry agents at the beginning of a pre-New Year's drive on alleged speakeasies and drinking resorts.

Thomas F. Gaughan and Thomas Guilfoyle, agents, entered the restaurant quietly and arrested Harry Moratta, 33 years old, and James De Marco, 30. Only a few patrons were in the place at the time. They were ordered to leave.

Trucks were summoned from Newark prohibition agents and reinforcements were sent to help the agents load the 1,000 cases. After several trips the seizure was stored in Newark headquarters and the agents took the prisoners to Hoboken Police Headquarters. They were released later under $1,000 bail for a hearing this morning before United States Commissioner Edward R. Stanton in Hoboken.

Stark's Restaurant, downtown dining place at 546 Pearl Street, was among fourteen alleged drinking resorts raided yesterday by agents of Andrew McCampbell, prohibition administrator, who seized supposed liquor in each place and took twenty-five prisoners.

The agents, after searching the place, found what they said was 250 bottles of liquor and two thirty-gallon barrels of wine. They arrested John Stein, headwaiter; Charles Horstig, cashier; Joseph Gauver, bartender, and Frank Schultz, Fritz Huber, Charles Brown, Max Basler, Matty Miller, Chris Keller, Frank Hero and Frank Meyer, waiters.

In a raid on the fifth floor of a loft building at 433-437 East Twenty-second Street the agents battered half an hour on a barred door before the barricade crashed down. When they entered the loft, they said, they found evidence that their would-be prisoners had escaped through one or more of several trapdoors in the floor or by way of a rear fire escape.

The agents were rewarded, however, by discovering a 2,000-gallon still in operation and forty-two 500-gallon vats of sugar mash. The still, they said, was heated electrically and all of the equipment, valued at $10,000, was of the most recent type. The agents reported the seizure there of 115 gallons of alcohol.

Mr. McCamphell's men seized small quantities of alleged beer, liquor and wine and arrested prisoners in raids on places at 906 St. Nicholas Avenue; 3,576 Broadway; 3,594 Broadway; 3,061 Webster Avenue, the Bronx; 512 East Eightieth Street; 2,999 Webster Avenue, the Bronx; 724 Amsterdam Avenue; 535 East 180th Street; 364 East 155th Street; 883 Eighth Avenue; 2,359 Webster Avenue; 3,640 Broadway.

Final Action at Capital; Proclaims the End of the Prohibition Law

BY THE NEW YORK TIMES | DEC. 6, 1933

WASHINGTON, DEC. 5 — Legal liquor today was returned to the United States, with President Roosevelt calling on the people to see that "this return of individual freedom shall not be accompanied by the repugnant conditions that obtained prior to the adoption of the Eighteenth Amendment and those that have existed since its adoption."

Prohibition of alcoholic beverages as a national policy ended at 5:32½ P. M., Eastern Standard Time, when Utah, the last of the thirty-six States, furnished by vote of its convention the constitutional majority for ratification of the Twenty-first Amendment. The new amendment repealed the Eighteenth, and with the demise of the latter went the Volstead Act which for more than a decade held legal drinks in America to less than one-half of 1 per cent of alcohol and the enforcement of which cost more than 150 lives and billions in money.

Earlier in the day Pennsylvania had ratified as the thirty-fourth State and Ohio as the thirty-fifth.

PROCLAMATION BY PRESIDENT.

President Roosevelt at 6:55 P.M. signed an official proclamation in keeping with terms of the National Industrial Recovery Act, under which prohibition ended and four taxes levied to raise $227,000,000 annually for amortization of the $3,300,000,000 public works fund were repealed.

But the President went further. Accepting certification from Acting Secretary of State Phillips that thirty-six States had ratified the repealing amendment, he improved the occasion to address a plea to the American people to employ their regained liberty first of all for national manliness.

Mr. Roosevelt asked personally for what he and his party had declined to make the subject of Federal mandate — that saloons be barred from the country.

"I ask especially," he said, "that no State shall, by law or otherwise, authorize the return of the saloon, either in its old form or in some modern guise."

MAKES PERSONAL PLEA.

He enjoined all citizens to cooperate with the government in its endeavor to restore a greater respect for law and order, especially by confining their purchases of liquor to duly licensed agencies. This practice, which he personally requested every individual and every family in the nation to follow, would result, he said, in a better product for consumption, in addition to the "break-up and eventual destruction of the notoriously evil illicit liquor traffic" and in tax benefits to the government.

The President thus announced the policy of his administration — to see that the social and political evils of the preprohibition era shall not be revived or permitted again to exist. Failure of citizens to use their new freedom in helping to advance this policy, he said, would be "a living reproach to us all."

He expressed faith, too, in the "good sense of the American people" in preventing excessive personal use of relegalized liquor. "The objective we seek through a national policy," he said, "is the education of every citizen toward a greater temperance throughout the nation."

As a means of enforcing his policy, the President has the Federal Alcohol Control Administration ready to take control of the liquor traffic and regulate it at the source of supply.

In its first major step today, the FACA moved to make available a better supply of whisky so that immediate heavy demands might not continue the bootlegging evil. The particular move was to establish an extra import quota for Canadian whiskies of American types, rye and bourbon, suitable for blending with; newer whiskies recently manufactured in this country.

A statement issued by the FACA read:

"A temporary liquor import committee, having regard for the special circumstances as to American bourbon and rye type which is suitable for

blending purposes, has decided to issue immediately permits for sub-stantial quotas of liquor of this category."

It was tacitly understood that practically all these "substantial quotas" would come from Canada.

Administration officials reiterated their confidence that the country would have an adequate supply of good liquors and wines within the next few days. Reports streamed into the FACA offices relative to the last-minute movements of liquor shipments to strategic wholesale points and every effort was being made to facilitate the issuance of import permits for the 4,800,000 gallons already allowed under foreign quotas.

WOULD PREVENT PROFITEERING.

The chief concern of officials relative to the supply was that profiteers should not reap the advantage of the immediate post-repeal demand, and that consumers, in resentment at higher prices, should not continue to patronize the bootlegger.

State Department officials, bent upon an appropriate ceremony for proclaiming the Twenty-first Amendment in effect, were taken somewhat aback when it was reported that Utah, determined to be the thirty-sixth State to ratify, would not act until about 9 P. M., Eastern standard time.

The Utah officials, according to advices reaching Washington, apparently had the idea that either Pennsylvania or Ohio might delay its convention a few hours so as to claim the distinction. However, when Pennsylvania certified its ratification before 1 o'clock and Ohio followed before 3, Utah had no further doubts.

Acting Secretary Phillips was at the White House at a meeting of the Executive Council when word reached his office that Utah would vote around 5 P.M. He hurried the last-minute preparations for the certification ceremony and had only a few minutes to wait before the telegraph wires in the State Department sounded the few ticks that told of prohibition's end.

While prohibition was thus ended nationally, many of the States remain dry and, doubtless, not a few will continue so. Only about a score had elected, up to this afternoon, to avail themselves of the new freedom allowed by the Twenty-first Amendment, although legislative processes are understood to be under contemplation in a number of others whereby liquor will be made legal.

TO PROTECT DRY STATES.

The new amendment makes it mandatory upon the Federal Government to protect these dry States from wet invasions.

Announcement was made at the Department of Justice this afternoon that the former force of 1,300 prohibition agents would be employed for the time being in that service. Attorney General Cummings changed the name of the force, however, from the Prohibition Division of the Bureau of Investigation to the Alcoholic Beverages Unit of the same bureau.

Legal divisions of a number of bureaus were still at work today making the adjustments necessary to repeal. Lawyers at the Industrial Alcohol Bureau, which passes tonight into the Bureau of Internal Revenue, said there would be no trouble about diverting stocks of medicinal liquor into commercial channels.

Repeal of the amendment carried with it repeal of the medicinal liquor laws, they said, adding that liquor sold in drugstores throughout the country, except in strictly Federal territory and States that forbid it, may be sold for beverage purposes. Concentration warehouses, they said, may release liquor to persons having permits to distribute it without any formal notice of repeal being sent to field agents.

DRY LEADERS' COMMENT.

At the final accomplishment of prohibition repeal today dry leaders hailed again their cause, with some of them predicting that the United States would return to some such method of liquor control.

In the absence from Washington of Dr. F. Scott McBride, general superintendent of the Anti-Saloon League of America, the following comment was made by O. G. Christgau, executive assistant:

"Legalized liquor is now on tap and also on trial. The people will render their verdict after they see the difference between prohibition and legalized liquor sales.

"From now on the sponsors of repeal must accept responsibility for the evils of liquor. It is up to them to try to keep their promises, and when they fail there will be a change. It is unfortunate for the wets that they won during hard times because liquor is bad enough in good times. Also it is tragic that repeal should have come just before Christmas.

"Repeal of the Eighteenth Amendment will not solve the liquor problem nor end the fight for prohibition. It's impossible to make liquor good by law and so long as the liquor traffic exists the battle against this intolerable evil will go on.

"By the time the Anti-Saloon League convention meets in Washington during the second week of January liquor sales systems will have been in effect in many of the States and there will have been a test of the promises to protect dry territory and keep out the saloons. The results will be reported and studied as a basis of a new dry program to combat the liquor evil.

"Meanwhile, the league insists that it is smarter not to drink at all than to drink legal liquor, especially if you drive an automobile."

CHAPTER 3

The Mid-20th Century

Turbulence reigned between the end of World War II and the late 1970s. Young men returned from the war scarred, scared and jobless. Immigrant populations boomed, constricted only by the size of the neighborhoods in which they were forced to live. Civil rights activists pushed for equal rights, and Vietnam war protesters called for peace. Drug addiction flared, as did police brutality, violent crime and property crimes. The "war on drugs" put hundreds of thousands of men — many of them black — behind bars.

Prison Population Seen Up After War

BY THE NEW YORK TIMES | NOV. 21, 1943

FIVE HUNDRED prison officials and correction workers from all parts of the country were told yesterday at the annual convention of the American Prison Association that they had better start thinking about the type of prisons to be built when the war ends, because of an expected large increase in the prison population, especially if there are economic dislocations.

The delegates heard also a plea for the immediate induction into the armed forces of as many qualified single inmates of penal institutions as possible, as a means of delaying the drafting of men with heavy family responsibilities. Col. Edward S. Shattuck, general counsel of the Selective Service System, criticized the Navy for refusing to accept ex-convicts.

Saying that about 90,000 men of military age were now in Federal and State jails and that perhaps 5,000 of the single men among them were suitable for immediate induction, Colonel Shattuck declared:

"If we can't do something with that manpower, then you gentlemen who are talking about doing something when the war is over are just talking through your hats. There never was a time in the history of the country when this manpower was needed more. If we can take these 5,000 men from the prisons, we'll have 5,000 honorable self-respecting men when the war is over and — more important — we can keep 5,000 married men with their families."

The post-war problems were discussed at a session presided over by James V. Bennett, director of the United States Bureau of Prisons. The convention, being held at the Hotel Pennsylvania, continues today and tomorrow.

Mr. Bennett said that the prison population had fallen from 170,000 to 130,000 since this country entered the war, but that it was sure to increase beyond the higher figure after the armed forces were demobilized and war industries ceased.

Dr. Thorsten Sellin of the University of Pennsylvania said that between 1923 and 1940 the nation's prison population increased seven times as fast as its general population and that this trend could be expected to resume after the war.

"As a result of the war our prison population has been falling," Professor Sellin said. "One reason is that the age group in which there has always been most crime has been drafted. Many of the prospective customers are in the armed forces. When the Army is demobilized, if accompanied by considerable economic dislocations, our prisons will be full again.

"We will probably have not only crowding of the old plants but a lack of construction during the war means we'll have to build lots more prisons after the war."

Mr. Bennett said that the various States had surpluses of $700,000,000 for post-war construction and said the Federal Government would probably make additional building funds available. Clarence Litchfield, a prison architect, discussed the merits and costs of different types of prisons.

Last night's session, after hearing a dozen adults discuss "juvenile delinquency and prevention" for nearly two hours, got the gist of the problem from a 14-year-old boy. "You have to go some place, so you go looking for trouble," explained Robert (Bobby) Linden, captain of "The Dukes," a club of forty-five boys on the upper West Side. "We wish we would get a few parks for recreation."

Bobby, who lives at 516 West 132d Street, was an unscheduled speaker. Discussing youthful gang wars, he said:

"You can't always find the right fellows, and you have to pick on some others. You need a little recreation. If you hang around the corners the police chase you away. But if we can't hang out there, we can't hang out no place. We go to cellars, and that leads us into temptation. You have to go some place, so you go looking for trouble."

Dr. J. Berkeley Gordon, medical director of the New Jersey State Hospital, Marlboro, N. J., urged that churches assume responsibility "for making parents assume proper care of their children."

A similar view was expressed by Judge Paul W. Alexander of Toledo, Ohio, president of the Association of Juvenile Court Judges of America, who declared that "juvenile delinquency is attributable to a breakdown in the morals of adults."

Crime Increasing in Little Spain

BY ALBERT J. GORDON | AUG. 3, 1947

THE AREA IN East Harlem known as "Little Spain," housing the Puerto Rican population, has been marked in the last eighteen months by a sharp increase in crime, especially among the teen-age population.

Police officials responsible for guarding the section from Fifth to First Avenues and from East Seventy-ninth to East 116th Streets described conditions there yesterday. They said the detectives and uniformed police working out of the East 104th and East 126th Street stations had had their hands full in trying to keep the crime rate down.

In "Little Spain" live the majority of the estimated 600,000 Puerto Ricans now in the United States. Puerto Rican officials challenge the estimate. They say not more than 350,000 are in this country.

Most of the Puerto Ricans in this city live in poverty, and are crowded into apartments, as many as fifteen or eighteen in four or five rooms. The situation is aggravated by the arrival of 2,000 or more Puerto Ricans by plane and ship every month. The majority remain in New York City. Some find employment. Others find their way on relief rolls. Being American citizens, the migrants don't need passports and are not involved in red tape.

BOY GANGS STAGE STICKUPS

The police in East Harlem said one of their greatest worries concerned the youngsters who organize themselves into gangs. Carrying crudely made pistols, the youngsters roam the streets during late night and early morning hours, engage in stick-ups and are not reluctant to fire.

Shopkeepers, mostly those who operate fruit stands, have complained frequently about daily pilferings. Although the police have maintained a careful watch, the robberies and hold-ups continue to increase. Purse-snatchings are common occurrences.

Another growing evil is the sale of narcotics. The use of habit-

Policemen patrolling the streets of East Harlem in the late 1940s.

forming drugs, the police said, is on the increase among the young as well as adults. The sale of marijuana cigarettes is increasing. The charge for a marijuana cigarette is $1. Not many can pay this price. For fifty cents the cigarette is cut in two, and the buyer gets one of the halves.

Various gambling games, such as dice, numbers and Spanish monte, are played day and night in back rooms.

POLICE STATION CROWDED

The police station at East 104th Street resembled last night the waiting room of a railroad station. Complainants, defendants, detectives and policemen marched in and out during all hours of the night.

The complaints ranged all the way from common assault and larceny to stabbings and shootings. The detectives and policemen deal on the spot with as many of the complaints as possible. Those requiring investigation keep piling up daily. The district presents problems unlike those in any other section of the city.

The East Harlem section has been the breeding ground for various forms of lotteries, in particular the policy-slip racket. This type of crime has become so evident that increased details of plainclothes policemen have been assigned to the area.

An increase in vice also has resulted in additional plainclothes details. Despite arrests and prosecution, prostitution continues. It is difficult to control and is reflected in the increasing number of cases of venereal disease reported by city health officials.

PLAYGROUNDS NEEDED

The police department has reported there is need for more supervised playrooms and play streets in the district. School windows have been broken and classrooms damaged as a result of unsupervised play in school yards. The absence of recreational centers and lack of parks, the police assert, is responsible for a good deal of the juvenile delinquency.

The police would like to see more coordinating councils like the one operating at the Wadleigh High School, which popularizes afternoon recreational activities especially designed for Puerto Ricans, and more cooperation with existing agencies.

The police would like to have more prominent Puerto Ricans participating in the coordinating councils. They want the schools to give greater publicity to the benefits of PAL, the Police Athletic League, which provides play activities for youngsters. The police also would like to see greater use of existing facilities to arouse public consciousness of Puerto Rican parents through Parent Teachers Associations, with addresses in Spanish, trips throughout the city and outlying areas through PAL auspices and the formation of more baseball and soccer teams.

23 More Undesirables
Are Seized in Times Square
as Round-Up Spreads

BY THE NEW YORK TIMES | AUG. 1, 1954

TWENTY-THREE new arrests were made in the Times Square area last night and early today as the police offensive against undesirables in the city's amusement district went into its second round. In the first series of raids, which began Friday night, more than one hundred persons were caught in the police net and fifty-eight of them were booked on disorderly conduct charges. The police said that the raids would go on in New York's trouble spots on a systematic basis as a part of the spreading campaign to rid the city of unsavory individuals in its streets. The second phase of the round-up operation last night was confined to street arrests although plainclothes men and uniformed patrolmen under Deputy Inspector George A. Neary, acting commander of the Third Division, concentrated their attentions on bars, grills and dance halls. Of the twenty-three persons arrested during the night, eighteen, including two women, were booked at the West Forty-seventh Street police station on disorderly conduct charges. Five others were charged with peddling without license. Six men of the first group pleaded guilty in Night Court early today and were fined $2 each, while six others pleaded innocent and were paroled for a later hearing. One of the immediate results of the police campaign appeared to be that many of the bars, usual hangouts of the undesirable persons, were oddly deserted last night in contrast to the normal Saturday crowds.

Chief Inspector Stephen P. Kennedy sent out orders yesterday morning to all uniformed policemen in the midtown area to be on the alert for persons annoying pedestrians. High police officials expressed themselves as satisfied that a start had been made toward ridding New York of its "undesirables," organized bands of youthful hoodlums and perverts.

"We are going to continue these raids in other trouble spots within the framework of civil liberties," one official said. Suspended thirty-day jail terms were handed out yesterday to eleven youths who pleaded guilty to disorderly conduct charges. Magistrate Nicholas F. Delagi, before whom forty-two were arraigned in Week-End Court, warned however that they would go to jail if they continued to be picked up.

"You're going to be picked up and picked up again, and you're going to go to jail," he told them. "The police are not picking up everyone — just those who don't belong up there [in the raided areas]."

Fifteen others also pleaded guilty, and five were fined $10 each and ten $5 each. Four others were remanded for hearings Aug. 10 in Probation Court; ten were held in $100 bail each for hearings Aug. 10 in the Court for Homeless Men and two in $100 each for hearings Tuesday in Lower Manhattan Court.

Sixteen appeared in Felony Court before Magistrate Thomas H. Cullen Jr. He quickly acquitted two 18-year-old stewards on the Holland-America liner Groote Beer. A Legal Aid Society lawyer said the youths, caught unwittingly in the raids, had started to run when a detective approached. They made their noon sailing from Hoboken.

Nine persons were held by Magistrate Cullen in $500 bail for a hearing tomorrow, one in $1,000 bail for a hearing Tuesday, and four in $500 each for a hearing the same day.

The raids followed similar forays, on a somewhat smaller scale, the previous Friday night. These took place in the Seventies and Eighties between Amsterdam and Columbus Avenues. Of the forty to fifty persons picked up, twenty-eight were held on disorderly conduct charges, and four for narcotics law violations.

Both round-ups were carefully planned and carried out by picked personnel. Squad commanders sent out detectives, dressed in the mode affected by the hoodlums, to make surveys and keep suspected places and "characters" under surveillance.

In the latest raids, thirty detectives under four squad commanders, augmented by other specialized squad personnel, concentrated on the area from Fortieth to Fifty-third Streets and from the Avenue of the Americas to Eighth Avenue. In charge of the operation both weeks was Deputy Chief Inspector James B. Leggett, who commands the detective bureau in Manhattan West.

The round-ups, the first of their kind in many years, followed complaints by the hundreds from merchants, civic leaders and out-of-town visitors. Hoodlums and perverts, roaming the streets at all hours and congregating in West Side bars, had made the Times Square sector unsafe, the complainants declared.

Inspector Leggett, in announcing that the raids were going to be continued, said that the rise of organized young hoodlums and the patent increase of homosexuals on the city's streets had brought a wave of rape, muggings and other crimes of violence often culminating in murder.

The inspector noted that, as in the case of ten youths who walked in a solid line on Broadway at Fifty-second Street and were subdued after a brief fight, the hoodlums wore a kind of uniform to show that they "belonged."

The youth usually wear T-shirts, blue dungarees and wide leather motorcycle belts ornamented with artificial, glittering "gems." That uniform has become almost standard, along with further aping of the motorcycle enthusiast's dress, such as short leather jackets and patent-leather peaked caps with white chin straps, and calf-high boots of the type worn by miners and engineers.

'Hot Summer' Race Riots in North

BY THE NEW YORK TIMES | JULY 26, 1964

Following years of peaceful civil rights protests in the South, frustration over the lack of progress in gaining equal rights, housing, job opportunities and wages resulted in the fomenting of more aggressive movements in both the South and the North. The spark of violence was ignited when a white off-duty police lieutenant killed a 15-year-old black boy in Brooklyn, New York.

SO, LAST WEEK, the "long hot summer" of Negro discontent began. In Harlem, in Brooklyn and upstate in Rochester there was rioting, shooting, charges and counter-charges. The race struggle had reached a climax and no immediate way out was indicated.

Thus, the issue had come violently to the North as it had to the South. The Civil Rights Bill had been enacted into law, but it became clear, in both areas of the nation, that much more than legislation was needed if the crisis were to be surmounted.

The uncertainty about the future was deepened by the fact that extremists, both of the left and the right, were ready to exploit Negro unrest for their own purposes. The moderates were having little success in their efforts to keep violence out of the struggle.

In addition, there were the political aspects. In the Presidential election campaign about to get under way, the race question is certain to play a large part. Senator Goldwater conferred with President Johnson last week and they agreed that "racial tension should be avoided."

But there was no indication that any such conference or any other measure now in prospect would lead to a quick diminution of Negro pressure or white backlash.

THE VIOLENCE

The contagion of racial violence last week began in Harlem, swept across the East River to the Bedford-Stuyvesant section of Brooklyn, flared back briefly to lower Manhattan, and then late in the week

New York State Police standing guard during the race riot in Rochester.

leaped 300 miles to Rochester.

Harlem, now one of the largest of the black ghettoes, was a well-to-do suburb at the turn of the century. Today its rundown brownstones and other tenements make it a vast slum. Extensive housing developments over the past 30 years have thinned its population somewhat (to about 400,000) and sent Negroes migrating to other ghettoes.

One such is Bedford-Stuyvesant, with a similar history of deterioration and blight and a population slightly smaller than Harlem's. Rochester, the state's third largest city (300,000), has about 35,000 Negroes.

The cycle of discrimination that confronts the Negro in these and other Northern ghettoes is hard to break. There is job discrimination, resulting in low Negro income. The low income plus housing discrimination condemn the Negro to living in the slums. There is apathy toward education, disqualifying many Negroes for many jobs that might otherwise be available. The bleakness of the Negro's future often puts him in conflict with the authority wielded by the dominant White man and breeds hostility toward the enforcer of that authority, the policeman.

The Northern Negro has relatively little to show for all the years of pressure against such discrimination. As a result the talk this year of a "long, hot summer" has grown. The potential for explosion was clearly there. Ten days ago came the spark.

It was struck by an incident in mid-Manhattan in which a 15-year-old boy, James Powell, was shot to death, by an off-duty police lieutenant, Thomas R. Gilligan. According to the police account, the boy had moved on the lieutenant with a knife and ignored a warning to stop. According to Negroes, he had no knife and the killing was unjustified.

PROTEST RALLY

The shooting sent a wave of intense indignation through the Negro community. A week ago last night the Congress of Racial Equality (CORE) held a protest rally in the heart of Harlem. Speakers excoriated the police. A preacher said it was time to act by marching to the police station two blocks away to demand Lieutenant Gilligan's suspension. The crowd moved off to cries of "Let's do it now!" At the station house they were confronted by a wall of policemen. Bottles and bricks began to rain down from the rooftops; the policemen put on steel helmets and fired their revolvers into the darkness, aiming over the heads of the missile-throwers. When a police captain told the Negroes to go home, a voice from the crowd screamed, "We are home, baby!"

Rapidly, the rioting spread to other areas of Harlem. Mobs — numbering now in the hundreds — swarmed through the streets. The barrage of bottles and bricks grew heavier; so did the police gunfire.

So began a week of wild disorders. This was the way it went:

Sunday. Again gangs roamed the streets of Harlem, taunting police, attacking whites, looting stores. More bottles and bricks were hurled, more shots were fired above the tenement rooftops.

Monday. There was new violence in Harlem; 17 persons were injured. For the first time, violence broke out In Bedford-Stuyvesant, where a CORE rally turned into a riot.

Tuesday. In Bedford-Stuyvesant there was large-scale looting as gangs broke into stores and shattered plate-glass windows. Two Negro men were shot by police; their wounds were described as critical. In Harlem, too, there was looting and fighting, but on a smaller scale.

Wednesday. In Brooklyn the tempo of violence mounted. Three Negro men — looters — were shot by police and 122 persons were injured. At least 200 stores were damaged.

PICKETS HARASSED

Thursday. A light rainfall seemed to cool tempers. In Harlem and in Bedford-Stuyvesant violence and looting were scattered and quickly halted. But trouble flared in a new area — at Police Headquarters in lower Manhattan, where hundreds of white youths jeered CORE pickets as they marched to protest alleged police brutality.

Friday. New York City was quiet, but in Rochester a full-scale race riot broke out after the arrest of a Negro during a street dance.

Saturday. The Rochester rioting continued; city officials declared a state of emergency and ordered an 8 P.M. curfew. Governor Rockefeller sent in 200 state troopers and alerted the National Guard. More than 80 persons were injured and the same number arrested. But last night rioting again broke out in Rochester. In Harlem, police broke up a planned protest parade by arresting the Communist who proposed to lead it.

From the week of violence these conclusions could be drawn:

First, the rioters were by no means a cross-section of the Negro communities. They were largely teen-agers and young men. As indicated by the looting, they included a substantial lawless element.

Second, the violence nevertheless reflected a mood of bitter protest that was general in the Negro communities — among those who stood on the sidewalks watching and jeering the police and those who stayed home as well as those who roamed the streets. Many Negroes deplored the violence but none denied that their grievances were real.

Third, the riots appeared to have no specific objective in furthering Negro rights other than the immediate one of protest against police "brutality." In Rochester an N.A.A.C.P. speaker was shouted down when she said: "Listen, listen ... what do you want?" The violence thus presented a sharp contrast to the non-violent, disciplined Negro demonstrations in the South with their clearly defined targets such as segregated lunch-counters and motels.

Fourth, the national Negro leadership was on the whole powerless to deal with the violence. What leadership was asserted on the side of pacification was mainly by local figures. During the week Roy Wilkins, executive Secretary of the National Association for the Advancement of Colored People, proposed a meeting of the heads of all civil rights organizations this week in an effort to reassert influence.

Fifth, there was evidence of organized direction to at least some of the disturbances. In Harlem some Negroes were observed carrying walkie-talkies; one of them said he was a CORE worker, but the organization denied it was using such equipment. Printed leaflets appeared telling how to make Molotov cocktails and attacking the police. The parade thwarted yesterday was called by the Harlem Defense Council, which has the same address as the Communist Progressive Labor Movement. There was also evidence of black nationalist influence. In Rochester the Black Muslim movement has been relatively strong.

THE RESPONSE

The question of incitement by extremists played an important part in efforts by local and Federal authorities to deal with the situation. Thus in Washington on Tuesday President Johnson announced that 200 F.B.I. agents were being sent to New York to study whether Federal laws were being violated. Mr. Johnson said:

"American citizens have a right to protection of life and limb — whether driving along a highway in Georgia, a road in Mississippi or a street in New York City."

Mayor Wagner, on his return from an interrupted European trip on Wednesday, broadcast an appeal for an end to the rioting, saying:

"Law and order are the Negroes' best friend. Make no mistake about that. The opposite of law and order is mob rule, and that is the way of the Ku Klux Klan and the night riders and the lynch mobs."

Mr. Wagner also said that F.B.I. director J. Edgar Hoover had given Police Commissioner Michael J. Murphy "certain information which is of the greatest interest and use."

At the same time, however, there was cautioning against hasty conclusions that the Negro discontent was not genuine and intense, regardless of whether extremists may have moved to exploit it for motives of their own.

As for the immediate causes of that discontent — the controversies over Lieutenant Gilligan in particular and alleged police brutality in general — those were left up in the air by the week's developments.

On Lieutenant Gilligan, the Negroes demanded that he be suspended from duty pending an investigation of the shooting of young Powell. Mr. Wagner pointed out that the lieutenant was on home leave because his hand was cut during the incident. And during the week District Attorney Frank Hogan began presenting evidence in the shooting of the Powell boy to a grand jury.

On charges of brutality, the Negroes have long demanded the creation of an independent civilian review board to examine specific charges against the police. Police Commissioner Murphy has strongly resisted any such outside supervision, saying the department's own Police Review Board could do the job. On Wednesday, with Mr. Murphy sitting at his side, the Mayor announced a step in the direction demanded by the Negroes. He said Deputy Mayor Edward F. Cavanagh Jr. would examine the Review Board's procedures and would inquire into all complaints sent to City Hall.

After the Mayor's speech, leaders of more than 50 Negro organizations met and said the Mayor's moves were not enough. In effect, they said: "Fire Murphy." This Mr. Wagner evidently was not prepared to do.

THE SOUTH

In the South, the focus last week was an effort to enforce the new Civil Rights Law, particularly in the Deep South. Thus in Atlanta the Civil Rights Act passed its first major test, as a three-judge Federal District Court unanimously ordered a hotel and a restaurant to comply with the public accommodations section of the law by Aug. 11. The delay was designed to give the owners of the establishments time to appeal to the Supreme Court, which both said they would do.

In Mississippi, the first arrests involving the Civil Rights Act were made last week in Greenwood. Three white men were charged by the F.B.I. with conspiring to violate the law. They were alleged to have beaten a Negro youth who had attended a previously all-white theater after its management agreed to admit Negroes. The defendants, under the law, are entitled to a jury trial.

In St. Augustine, site of racial conflict for two months, there was new violence by segregationists last week. Early Friday morning, as members of the Ku Klux Klan gathered for a rally near the city, a fire bomb was thrown into a restaurant that desegregated following passage of the civil rights law; the establishment was heavily damaged. The next day five men — all allegedly Klansmen — were arrested and charged with burning a cross on the property of a local bakery.

THE FUTURE

Is there a solution for the problems underlying last week's racial violence?

The problem in the North is different from that in the South. In the

South, the discrimination the Negro seeks to overcome takes relatively crude forms such as keeping him out of places of public accommodation and preventing him from registering to vote. And there is now a Federal law designed to bring these barriers down — the Civil Rights Act of 1964.

The new law, it is true, is being resisted in the hard-core segregationist regions of the Deep South, and the resistance is often expressed by white terrorism. But the die-hard area is shrinking. Over wide regions of the South the civil rights law is being complied with more readily than most Negro leaders had dared hope.

In the North, where the Negro's right to public accommodation and the unrestricted ballot has long been a matter of local law, the act passed by Congress July 2 has little relevance. Here it is a question of raising the economic, social and cultural level of a whole section of the population. And that, experts agree, would require efforts and expenditures on the Federal, state and local levels of a greater magnitude than any made or planned thus far.

WHITES THE KEY

Will the necessary measures be taken? To a large extent this probably will be determined by prevailing opinion within the political, social and religious groups of what the Negro leaders have come to call the "white power structure." Among whites in general there has been considerable sympathy with the Negro cause — an attitude reflected in the big majority in Congress for the civil rights bill; the increasing efforts by Northern cities with black ghettoes to provide Negroes with better education, job training and other aid; and the special attention given Negroes in the Administration's antipoverty program. All these actions represent a start.

Along with white sympathy and support, however, has come white resentment as Negro pressures have mounted against discrimination in housing and jobs maintained in the North by custom rather than by law. This "backlash" has been most pronounced among whites who are only a rung above the Negroes in economic status and who are anxious about Negro competition, about the value of their homes — now about the safety of the streets where they live.

The question facing the moderate Negro leaders thus is whether demonstrations and pressure that may lead to violence will hurt their cause by intensifying the backlash. The comments of some such leaders last week indicated that they are deeply concerned over this danger. What is not clear is what they plan to do — or can do — to prevent violence within a mass movement they do not completely control.

THE POLITICS

The Johnson-Goldwater meeting last week had a strictly limited objective — agreement on steps to avoid inflaming racial tensions during the campaign. There was no talk on either side of keeping the race question out of politics. It was recognized that race had become inextricably intertwined with politics the moment that Senator Goldwater, an opponent of the Civil Rights Act of 1964, was nominated.

The meeting came about almost by chance. Early in the week, during an informal news conference, a reporter asked Mr. Goldwater whether he would be willing to meet the President in an effort to avoid Inflammatory debate. The Senator replied that he would like to reach an "agreement that we or our associates would not, in any word we might say, add to the feelings of tension that exist today."

At the White House, Press Secretary George Reedy said he was certain Mr. Johnson would give "serious consideration" to any such proposal. On Thursday Mr. Goldwater's staff asked the White House for an appointment for the Senator. The time was set for late Friday afternoon.

The two men met for 16 minutes. Afterward the White House issued a statement to which Mr. Goldwater had agreed. The complete statement said:

"The President met with Senator Goldwater and reviewed the steps he had taken to avoid the incitement of racial tension. Senator

Goldwater expressed his opinion, which was that racial tension should be avoided. Both agreed on this position."

Actually neither Senator nor President could keep the civil rights issue out of the campaign if he tried, and both said as much during the week, On Monday Mr. Goldwater, bringing up the issue, said, "That's kind of hard to do unless you lock them up in a room and throw the key away."

Mr. Johnson, at a news conference two hours before his meeting with the Senator, emphatically dismissed the notion that civil rights could be excluded from the campaign debates. He said:

"I believe that all men and women are entitled to equal opportunities .... Now, to the extent that Senator Goldwater differs from these views, or the Republican party differs, there will, of course, be discussion. And I intend to carry on some of it if I am a candidate."

Moreover, the campaign as a whole is expected to turn on the extent of the so-called "white backlash" against integration pressures. Senator Goldwater's strategy clearly is based on the hope of capturing "backlash" votes. The prospect is that many Southern segregationists will support him.

Mr. Goldwater's strategy also involves the risk that he will lose most if not all of the big states of the Northeastern section of the country, where the Negro and other integrationist vote is substantial. But some observers feel this risk may not be so great as might be expected. The white backlash is in evidence in the North also, as indicated by the sizable votes for Governor Wallace in the Indiana and Wisconsin primaries. Many observers believe it was reinforced as a result of the Negro rioting in New York last week.

But this white reaction against the integrationists appears to be in large measure a silent protest. Perhaps its full weight will not become clear until the voters go to the polls Nov. 3.

Narcotics Drive Raises Arrests

BY WILLIAM BORDERS | OCT. 13, 1964

THE NUMBER OF narcotics arrests in New York City has risen sharply since Police Commissioner Michael J. Murphy declared an "all-out war" on illegal drug traffic last month.

The head of the Narcotics Bureau said the increase in arrests, both by his men and by other members of the police force, was "definitely" a result of the crackdown. Another result has been a large increase in the illegal price of narcotics.

Inspector Ira Bluth, the bureau commander, said yesterday that one grain of adulterated heroin, which sold for $3 last month, was now selling for about $5.

The price increase is thought to reflect a shortage resulting from caution on the part of narcotics pushers, rather than any general shortage of supply. Inspector Bluth said the addict "finds it harder to get the stuff because many of the low-level pushers have either been arrested or had their supplies cut off from above by bigger pushers who are afraid of the law."

HARMFUL EFFECT SEEN

Some police officials have cited the narcotics crackdown as a cause of a variety of other crimes, including two murders in the last week; in each case detectives quoted the murder suspect as saying he had killed his dope pusher because the pusher had started selling drastically diluted heroin.

The Police Department's general crime statistics do not show any sharp rise in muggings and robberies since Commissioner Murphy intensified his drive against narcotics. But Inspector Bluth and others said that such a rise could ultimately be expected if addicts suddenly needed more money to support their narcotics habits.

The inspector's 200-man squad made 654 narcotics arrests last month, an increase of 23 per cent over August and of 55 per cent over September 1963.

Narcotics arrests by the rest of the force totaled 773. This was 7 per cent more than the figure for August and 94 per cent more than the total for September 1963.

9-MONTH TOTAL RISES

The total of narcotics arrests by the entire force for the first nine months of this year is 54 per cent higher than the figure for the same period last year.

"The increased arrests by men outside my office are especially gratifying," Inspector Bluth said, "because we have been trying hard to make the rest of the force more conscious of the narcotics problem."

Steps to widen the drive against the narcotics traffic were outlined by Commissioner Murphy Sept. 9 at a meeting of 300 of the city's highest-ranking police officers.

The steps include a two-day training session given by the Narcotics Bureau to 700 plain-clothes men, who normally work on gambling and vice, and to the 400 members of the Youth Division.

"The object here is to take the specialty out of narcotics work, and to make the pusher the target of every police officer in the city," Inspector Bluth said.

Warring on Crime

OPINION | BY THE NEW YORK TIMES | FEB. 16, 1965

A COUNTEROFFENSIVE against the rising crime rate in all big cities seems at last to be under way. President Johnson has proposed imaginative new approaches for use in Washington, D. C. Mayor Wagner has ordered the New York police to study new ways of combating crime at the same time that he has authorized more policemen for both general and subway duty.

The President has recognized that, important as it is to have an adequate police force, experimentation also is needed in curing the "maladjustments which lead to crime." Little real safety for society is provided by a system in which the same people pop up over and over as the perpetrators of crimes. Narcotics addiction has become perhaps the greatest font of criminal behavior; yet it is plain that treating addiction through police tactics alone provides no beginnings of a solution.

The men Mayor Wagner proposes to add to the New York police force will cost the city $9 or $10 million. It is a worthwhile and necessary expense. But the expansion in police protection will never be enough unless parallel progress can be made in striking at the roots of crime and in putting tighter curbs on guns and other deadly weapons.

As the President rightly said, "We cannot tolerate an endless, self-defeating cycle of imprisonment, release and reimprisonment which fails to alter undesirable attitudes and behavior."

Johnson Presses Anticrime Drive

BY FRED P. GRAHAM | MARCH 10, 1966

WASHINGTON, MARCH 9 — President Johnson, citing the costs in death, suffering, fear and dollars, called today for greater efforts and ingenuity in the war on crime.

In his second annual message to Congress on crime, the President condemned "years of public neglect" and repeated his endorsement of several major anticrime measures that have not yet been approved by Congress, and added several new ones.

Both old and new programs perpetuate his basic policy of leaving the responsibility for crime control in local hands, with Federal assistance primarily to stimulate local experimentation, research and experimentation, research and exchange of information.

Mr. Johnson's 1965 crime measures did not fare well in Congress, and his message today was in the nature of let's-get-on-wlth-it.

He pointed to the current pace of crime that "marks the life of every American — a forcible rape every 26 minutes — a robbery every five minutes — an aggravated assault every three minutes — a car theft every minute — a burglary every 28 seconds."

'NATION OF CAPTIVES'

Mr. Johnson said a truly free people could not tolerate a fear of crime "that can turn us into a nation of captives imprisoned nightly behind chained doors, double locks, barred windows — fear that can make us afraid to walk city streets by night or public parks by day."

New proposals suggested by the President include:

• An increase from $7.2-million to $l3.7-million in annual Federal support for local experimental programs to improve police training and develop new techniques. An award program would be set up for police officers who produce new law enforcement ideas.

• A commission of outstanding lawyers, judges, Government officials and Congressmen to recommend at total revision of Federal criminal laws by 1968.

• The centralization of all probation officers under the Department of Justice. They are now appointed and controlled by the individual Federal District Courts.

• New laws to send about 3,000 police officers to college each year for a year of professional study, and a loan forgiveness program for students who wish to enter law enforcement as a profession.

• A new program to make Labor Department job information available to "good risk" parolees and to "deal fairly and sensibly with them" in Federal employment.

• Establishment of clinics to help train local law enforcement officials in narcotics problems in cities where addiction is most prevalent. A high Government official mentioned New York, Chicago, Los Angeles and Detroit as probable sites for some of these clinics.

Mr. Johnson said a second stage in the anticrime effort centered on the National Crime Commission, which is now engaged in some 40 projects with state and local authorities.

He emphasized the commission's efforts to employ modern science to better advantage in law enforcement.

"Modern electronics has made it possible to summon a doctor from his seat at the opera," he said. "Surely it can do as much to make police instantly responsible to public needs."

PRECINCT STUDIES SET

Justice Department officials disclosed today that a new commission study of "precinct profiles" would take teams of experts into selected precincts of New York, Chicago and Washington for elaborate background analyses of crime.

Team members will be on duty around the clock to record and study every crime. Results will be compared with the Federal Bureau of Investigation's statistics as a check on their accuracy.

TO WORK WITH STATES

Mr. Johnson said he had instructed Attorney General Nicholas deB. Katzenbaoh to work with the governors of the 50 states to establish state crime commissions.

They will work with the national commission to "undertake detailed planning of their own for reforms that take account of their own special strengths, needs and traditions."

A third phase of the anticrime drive rests upon the national commitment to social justice and personal dignity, the President said.

He emphasized the need for fair and speedy court administration, improved bail procedures and better sentencing procedures.

"The war on crime will be waged by our children and our children's children," he said and, continued:

"But the difficulty and complexity of the problem cannot be permitted to lead us to despair. They must lead us rather to bring greater efforts, greater ingenuity and greater determination to do battle."

Police Battle Demonstrators in Street; Hundreds Injured

BY J. ANTHONY LUKAS | AUG. 29, 1968

Dozens of demonstrations protesting the U.S. military operations in Vietnam were held throughout the 1960s and early 1970s. Initially peaceful, this anti-war rally outside the Democratic National Convention in 1968 turned violent when police used brute force to dispel the activists. The organizers, called the Chicago Seven, were later indicted for conspiracy, inciting riots and other protest-related charges. There were both convictions and acquittals in the case, but in the end, all convictions were reversed.

CHICAGO, THURSDAY, AUG. 29 — The police and National Guardsmen battled young protesters in downtown Chicago last night as the week-long demonstrations against the Democratic National Convention reached a violent and tumultuous climax.

About 100 persons, including 25 policemen, were injured and at least 178 were arrested as the security forces chased down the demonstrators. The protesting young people had broken out of Grant Park on the shore of Lake Michigan in an attempt to reach the International Amphitheatre where the Democrats were meeting, four miles away.

UNEASY CALM

Shortly after midnight, an uneasy calm ruled the city. However, 1,000 National Guardsmen were moved back in front of the Conrad Hilton to guard it against more than 5,000 demonstrators who had drifted back into Grant Park.

The crowd in front of the hotel was growing, booing vociferously every time new votes for Vice President Humphrey were broadcast from the convention hall.

The events in the streets stirred anger among some delegates at the convention. In a nominating speech Senator Abraham A. Ribicoff of Connecticut told the delegates that if Senator George S. McGovern were President, "we would not have these Gestapo tactics in the

Police swing nightsticks, attempting to clear demonstrators from Chicago's Grant Park.

streets of Chicago." When Mayor Richard J. Daley of Chicago and other Illinois delegates rose shouting angrily, Mr. Ribicoff said, "How hard it is to accept the truth."

CRUSHED AGAINST THE WINDOWS

Even elderly bystanders were caught in the police onslaught. At one point, the police turned on several dozen persons standing quietly behind police barricades in front of the Conrad Hilton Hotel watching the demonstrators across the street.

For no reason that could be immediately determined, the blue-helmeted policemen charged the barriers, crushing the spectators against the windows of the Haymarket Inn, a restaurant in the hotel. Finally the window gave way, sending screaming middle-aged women and children backward through the broken shards of glass.

The police then ran into the restaurant and beat some of the victims who had fallen through the windows and arrested them.

At the same time, other policemen outside on the broad, tree-lined avenue were clubbing the young demonstrators repeatedly under television lights and in full view of delegates' wives looking out the hotel's windows.

Afterward, newsmen saw 30 shoes, women's purses and torn pieces of clothing lying with shattered glass on the sidewalk and street outside the hotel and for two blocks in each direction.

It was difficult for newsmen to estimate how many demonstrators were in the streets of midtown Chicago last night. Although 10,000 to 15,000 young people gathered in Grant Park for a rally in the afternoon, same of them had apparently drifted home before the violence broke out in the evening.

Estimates of those involved in the action in the night ranged between 2,000 and 5,000.

Although some youths threw bottles, rocks, stones and even loaves of bread at the police, most of them simply marched and countermarched, trying to avoid the flying police squads.

Some of them carried flags — the black anarchist flag, the red flag, the Vietcong flag and the red and blue flags with a yellow peace symbol.

STAYED DEFIANT

Although clearly outnumbered and outclassed by the well-armed security forces, the thousands of antiwar demonstrators, supporters of Senator Eugene J. McCarthy and Yippies maintained an air of defiance throughout the evening.

They shouted "The streets belong to the people," "This land is our land" and "Hell no, we won't go," as they skirmished along the avenue and among the side streets.

When arrested youths raised their hands in the V for victory sign that has become a symbol of the peace movement, other demonstrators shouted "Sieg heil" or "Pigs" at the policemen making the arrests.

Frank Sullivan, the Police Department's public information director, said the police had reacted only after "50 hard-core leaders" had staged a charge into a police line across Michigan Avenue.

Mr. Sullivan said that among those in the charge were Prof. Sidney Peck, cochairman of the Mobilization Committee to End the War in Vietnam, the group that is spearheading the demonstration. He said Professor Peck had struck James M. Rochford, Deputy Superintendent of Police, with his fist. Mr. Peck was arrested and charged with aggravated assault.

As the night wore on, the police dragnet spread from Michigan Avenue and the area around the Hilton throughout downtown Chicago.

On the corner of Monroe Street and Michigan Avenue, policemen chased demonstrators up the steps of the Chicago Art Institute, a neo-classical Greek temple, and arrested one of them.

As in previous nights of unrest here, newsmen found themselves special targets of the police action. At Michigan Avenue and Van Buren Street, a young photographer ran into the street, terrified, his hands clasped over his head and shrieking "Press, press!"

As the police arrested him, he shouted, "What did I do? What did I do?" The policeman said, "If you don't know you shouldn't be a photographer."

Barton Silverman, a photographer for the New York Times, was briefly arrested near the Hilton Hotel.

Bob Kieckhefer, a reporter for United Press International, was hit in the head by a policeman during the melee in front of the Hilton. He staggered into the UPI office on Michigan Avenue and was taken for treatment to Wesley Memorial Hospital.

REPORTERS HAMPERED

Reporters and photographers were repeatedly hampered by the police last night while trying to cover the violence. They were herded into small areas where they could not see the action. On Jackson Street, police forced a mobile television truck to turn off its lights.

Among those arrested was the Rev. John Boyles, Presbyterian chaplain at Yale and a McCarthy staff worker, who was charged with breach of the peace.

"It's an unfounded charge," Mr. Boyles said. "I was protesting the clubbing of a girl I knew from the McCarthy staff. They were beating her on her head with clubs and I yelled at them 'Don't hit a woman,' At that point I was slugged in the stomach and grabbed by a cop who arrested me."

Last night's violence broke out when hundreds of demonstrators tried to leave Grant Park after a rally and enter the Loop area.

At the Congress Street bridge leading from the park onto Michigan Avenue, National Guardsmen fired and sprayed tear gas at the demonstrators five or six times around 7 P.M. to hold them inside the park.

However, one group moved north inside the park and managed to find a way out over another bridge. There they met a contingent of the Poor People's Campaign march led by their symbol, three mule wagons.

CHASE YOUTHS

The march was headed south along Michigan Avenue and the police did not disrupt it, apparently because it had a permit. But they began chasing the youths along Michigan Avenue and into side streets.

The demonstrators were then joined by several thousand others who had originally set out from the park in a "nonviolent" march to the amphitheatre led by David Dellinger, national chairman of the Mobilization Committee to End the War in Vietnam, and Allen Ginsberg, the poet.

The climactic day of protests began with a mass rally sponsored by the mobilization committee in the band shell in Grant Park.

The rally was intended both as a mass expression of anger at the proceedings across town in the convention and as a "staging ground" for the smaller, more militant march on the amphitheatre.

However, before the rally was an hour old, it, too, was interrupted by violence. Fighting broke out when three demonstrators started hauling down an American flag from a pole by the park's band shell where speakers were denouncing the Chicago authorities, the Johnson administration and the war in Vietnam.

Four blue-helmeted policemen moved in to stop them and were met by a group of angry demonstrators who pushed them back against a cluster of trees by the side of the band shell. Then the demonstrators, shouting "Pig, pig," pelted the isolated group of 14 policemen with stones, bricks, and sticks.

GRENADE HURLED BACK

Snapping their Plexiglass shields down over their faces, the police moved toward the crowd. One policeman threw or fired a tear-gas grenade into the throng. But a demonstrator picked up the smoking grenade and heaved it back among the police. The crowd cheered with surprise and delight.

But then, from the Inner Drive west of the park, a phalanx of policemen moved into the crowd, using their billy clubs as prods and then swinging them. The demonstrators, who replied with more stones and sticks were pushed back against rows of flaking green benches and trapped there.

Among those injured was Rennie Davis, one of the coordinators for the Mobilization Committee to End the War in Vietnam, which has been spearheading the demonstrations in Chicago.

As the police and demonstrators skirmished on the huge grassy field, mobilization committee leaders on the stage of the baby-blue band shell urged the crowd to sit down and remain calm.

The worst of the fighting was over in 10 minutes, but the two sides were still jostling each other all over the field when Mr. Ginsberg approached the microphone.

Speaking in a cracked and choking voice, Mr. Ginsberg said, "I lost my voice chanting in the park the last few nights. The best strategy for you in cases of hysteria, overexcitement or fear is still to chant 'Om' together. It helps to quell flutterings of butterflies in the belly. Join me now as I try to lead you."

So, as the policemen looked out in astonishment through their Plexiglass face shields, the huge throng chanted the Hindu "Om, om," sending deep mystic reverberations off the glass office towers along Michigan Avenue.

Following Mr. Ginsberg to the microphone was Jean Genet, the French author. His bald head glistening in the glare of television lights, Mr. Genet said through a translator, "It took an awful lot of deaths in Hanoi for a happening such as is taking place here to occur."

Next on the platform was William Burroughs, author of "The Naked Lunch." A gray fedora on his head, Mr. Burroughs said in a dry, almost distant voice, "I've just returned from London, England, where there is no effective resistance at all. It's really amazing to see people willing to do something about an unworkable system. It's not evil or immoral, just unworkable. And they're trying to make it work, by force. But they can't do it."

MAILER APOLOGIZES

Mr. Burroughs was followed by Norman Mailer, the author who is here to write an article on the convention. Mr. Mailer, who was arrested during the march on the Pentagon last October, apologized to the crowd for not marching in Chicago. Thrusting his jaw into the microphone, he said: "I'm a little sick about all this and also a little mad, but I've got a deadline on a long piece and I'm not going to go out and march and get arrested, I just came here to salute all of you."

Then Dick Gregory, the comedian and Negro militant leader, took the platform. Dressed in a tan sport shirt and matching trousers with a khaki rain hat on his head, Mr. Gregory said: "You just have to look around you at all the police and soldiers to know you must be doing something right."

Many of the demonstrators in Grant Park had drifted down in small groups from Lincoln Park, where 300 policemen had moved in at 12:15 A.M yesterday and laid down a barrage of tear gas to clear the area. About 2,000 young protesters had attempted to stay in the park despite an 11 P.M. curfew.

Militants Vow to Continue Protest at Harlem Church

BY THE NEW YORK TIMES | JAN. 4, 1970

MILITANT YOUNG Puerto Ricans who seized a Methodist church in East Harlem last Sunday vowed yesterday to continue their occupation until the police forcefully removed them or until church officials agreed to let them run a breakfast program for children there.

Their refusal to vacate the First Spanish Methodist Church at 163 East 111th Street was a repetition of their answer the night before to a court order from State Supreme Court Justice Hyman Korn.

"We are all presently in contempt of court — all of us, including you press men," said Juan Gonzalez, the minister of education and health for the group, the Young Lords, at news conference held in the morning in the church's basement.

BARRIER TO CITY NOTED

"Why then have we not been arrested?" continued Mr. Gonzalez. "Because the power of the Puerto Rican community outside of the church and the 300 people that occupied the church last night are preventing the city from moving against us."

The seizure of the church last week came after the Young Lords, who fashion themselves as a kind of Puerto Rican equivalent to the Black Panthers, had been demanding that the church allow them to use its facilities to operate a free breakfast program for neighborhood children.

"If they had granted us the space in the first place," said David Perez, the Lords' minister of defense, "we wouldn't have had to go through all this business."

After the militants took over the church, Captain Arthur Bailer of the police said church officials had not asked him to intercede. He said that the church would seek the removal of the occupants by court injunctions.

With the Lords refusal to leave despite Justice Korn's order, the next step is up to the church to secure a citation of contempt from the court, New York City's acting sheriff said yesterday.

H. Williams Kehl, the acting sheriff, added that the church could request such a citation from Justice Korn at any time and thus lead the way to the militants' removal by the sheriff, acting on behalf of the court, with the help of police.

Neither Justice Korn nor officials of the church were available yesterday for discussion of their plans.

During the news conference yesterday, supporters and friends of the Young Lords, moved freely in and out of the church. Children were busy playing handball in a small gymnasium on the first floor.

Mr. Perez and Mr. Gonzalez, 20 and 22 years of age, respectively, promised not to use violence in response to removal by the police, but added they would feel compelled to defend themselves "if we have to."

In a previous confrontation with the police, 14 persons were arrested last Dec. 7 after the Young Lords interrupted a church service to press their demands.

Negroes Held Oppressed by the Law

BY EARL CALDWELL | AUG. 1, 1971

SAN FRANCISCO, JULY 31 — After a year of study, a prominent black lawyer has concluded that the criminal process is being used across the country to contain blacks and the poor.

The lawyer, Herbert O. Reid, said in an interview: "To a great extent, the criminal law is being used as the first line of defense, the first area of governmental concern in enforcing governmental policy."

Mr. Reid, a professor of law at Howard University in Washington, is staff director of a commission established late in 1969 for a national study of clashes between the police and the Black Panther party. He said the situation had reached "a grave, grave magnitude."

Mr. Reid took over as director of the commission of inquiry in June 1970.

UNIT FORMED BY 30

The commission was formed by more than 30 prominent citizens in civil rights, law, politics and business. The prime movers were Roy Wilkins, executive director of the National Association for the Advancement of Colored People, and Arthur J. Goldberg, former Associate Justice of the Supreme Court.

Besides the police–Panther confrontation, the commission is looking into the administration of justice as it pertains to blacks and other minorities.

Mr. Reid said that he had found increasing pressure to relax procedural safeguards and due process standards to take care of the increased load on the criminal process from arrest through incarceration.

"If you look at the arrest records, they're increasing. If you look at incarceration, it's increasing, and yet there is greater agitation on the part of the Government, with great support from the public sector to facilitate this process," he said.

TRAGEDY SEEN

"One of the tragic things about it is that you're talking about blacks and the poor, and they are not having one damn bit of input in how they are to be put in jail and kept in jail," he added.

Mr. Reid, in explaining his conclusions, said that the disparate conditions of the affluent and the poor in the country were such that "it appears to me that there is no realistic policy and program to close this gap, to increase the hopes and aspirations of the blacks and the poor, but to use the criminal process to hold the line and to contain."

Mr. Reid said recent utterances of Attorney General John N. Mitchell and Chief Justice Warren E. Burger were evidence of the Government's policy. He said they had offered suggestions that would in effect "speed and short circuit the criminal process."

"If you follow that line, you could end up exterminating some people you dislike. When you end up, it's the cheapest thing to do," he said.

HAMPTON DEATH STUDIED

The commission has made a detailed study of the fatal shooting by the Chicago police of Fred Hampton, a Panther leader.

Mr. Reid said the staff report on the killing of Mr. Hampton had been completed and was in the hands of the commission. That report is expected to be made public in the near future.

Mr. Reid and his aides have observed the trial of Huey P. Newton, the Panther leader who is on trial in Oakland for the fatal shooting of a policeman. They also sat in on pretrial hearings involving Angela Davis, the former University of California philosophy instructor who has been indicted on charges of murder, kidnapping and criminal conspiracy. Mr. Reid also met with Bobby Seale, the chairman of the Black Panther party, who was recently involved in trials in Chicago and New Haven.

"A kind of repressive period is upon us and gaining momentum," Mr. Reid said.

He said that the law and order movement had gained respectability, financial assistance, the stamp of governmental approval and some evidence of popular support and that it was "doing some alarming things to the criminal process."

He was also critical of the police and the courtroom conduct of certain prosecutors. He said that he was wary of the growth of police departments as independent political powers.

He said that there was too much inbreeding in the administration of criminal justice between prosecutors and public officials.

"After a while," he said, "these people begin to approach their task with a missionary zeal. They begin to feel as though they are about God's business."

He said open animosity existed in the courtroom.

"They do not have a dispassionate approach," he said. "You get the feeling that they would try any method, fair or foul, with the notion that if we don't get you today, we'll get you tomorrow."

President Calls for 'Total War' on U.S. Addiction

BY JAMES M. MARKHAM | MARCH 21, 1972

PRESIDENT NIXON met here for three hours yesterday with Governor Rockefeller, law-enforcement officials, judges and narcotics rehabilitation specialists, and then called for "total war" on drug addiction.

Calling drug addiction the nation's domestic "public enemy No. 1," Mr. Nixon — though making no major policy statements — indicated in impromptu remarks that he placed high hopes on a law-enforcement approach.

"For those who traffic in drugs, for those who, for example, make hundreds of thousands of dollars — and sometimes millions of dollars — and thereby destroy the lives of our young people throughout this country, there should be no sympathy whatever and no limit insofar as the criminal penalty is concerned," said the President, who recently ordered a nationwide campaign against street pushers.

ATTACK ON HEROIN PUSHERS

Ronald L. Ziegler, the President's press secretary, explained later that the President meant by this remark that heroin pushers should be prostrated to the fullest extent now possible under current law.

"In the whole field of criminal law, this has the highest priority of this Administration," the President told Myles J. Ambrose, the new special assistant attorney general who will head the attack on street pushers.

Mr. Nixon, who landed at Kennedy International Airport at 10:40 A.M. and flew by helicopter to the Wall Street Heliport, was driven to 26 Federal Plaza in downtown Manhattan. There, wearing no overcoat, he greeted several hundred amiable civil servants who had gathered in the sunshine outside the building.

President Nixon with Governor Rockefeller during a conference in 1972 about the campaign against drug abuse.

CONFERENCE HELD

The President immediately went into conference with Mr. Ambrose and others involved with the new Office of Drug Abuse Law Enforcement, which will attempt to coordinate Federal, state and local resources to bring heroin retailers to trial. The first of nine regional offices of the agency was recently set up at 26 Federal Plaza.

Mr. Ambrose told the President that he hoped to coordinate his own law-enforcement efforts with the treatment and rehabilitation programs being mounted by Dr. Jerome Jaffe, head of the Special Action Office for Drug Abuse Prevention, so that addicts are driven off the streets and into treatment programs.

Mr. Nixon, in several remarks during his visit, also stressed that the Administration's approach to addiction combined both law enforcement and treatment.

The visit to New York was seen by many as part of an effort to refocus public attention on the President's domestic concerns after his historic visit to China. But Mr. Nixon several times spoke of China and its historic opium problem.

In preparing himself for the China visit, Mr. Nixon said, he was struck by the fact that, historically, Chinese politicians of varying ideologies had agreed that "the most reprehensible legacy" of European colonialism in China was opium smoking.

He noted that the Chinese Communists had not tolerated "permissiveness" and had taken a "hard line" on opium addiction, although he conceded that it was easier for a "totalitarian" nation like China to deal with narcotics addiction than it was for the United States.

"Any nation that moves down the road to addiction," Mr. Nixon cautioned later in the day, "that nation has something taken out of its character."

Mr. Nixon praised the "guts" of the Turkish Government of Premier Nihat Erim, with whom he will have talks in Washington today, and said that Turkey would soon be "out of the heroin market" as a result of an agreement with the United States.

Although the Turkish Government agreed last June to halt the growing of opium poppies at the end of this spring's harvest and the United States agreed to supply $35-million to help farmers switch to other crops, the decision has been highly unpopular in Turkey.

Last month Premier Erim told a meeting of agricultural engineers in Ankara that the ban had caused serious economic hardship and might have to be reconsidered.

After his meeting with Mr. Ambrose and others involved in the street-pusher campaign, Mr. Nixon sat down yesterday with Governor Rockefeller and officials and several judges involved in the running of eight special narcotics courts here.

The courts have been financed by a $7.5-million Federal Law Enforcement Assistance Administration grant and $2.5-million in matching state money. Four more narcotics courts will be set up in the city.

Mr. Nixon said the special narcotics courts were a prototype that, if successful, could spread "across the country."

Governor Rockefeller repeatedly expressed his thanks to President Nixon for the Federal funds to establish the special narcotics courts.

"You have made this possible, Mr. President," Mr. Rockefeller said.

After his meeting with Governor Rockefeller, Mr. Nixon paid a hasty visit at 26 Federal Plaza to a dozen narcotics undercover men and then was flown by Army helicopter to Kennedy Airport, where he visited customs officials in the East Wing of the International Arrivals Building.

The President chatted briefly with eight customs inspectors — who had been singled out for having personally intercepted smuggled marijuana or heroin — as well as with startled passengers who had just debarked from Pan American Flight 101 from London.

"More money will be needed in the future, and more money will be available," the President said, noting that his Administration had increased expenditures on drug programs almost sevenfold — to $600 million for fiscal year 1973. "We must have no budget cuts in waging total war on public enemy No. 1."

Mr. Nixon returned to Washington at 1:35 P.M. aboard a Boeing 707 that serves as a back-up jet for "The Spirit of '76," which is undergoing a spring overhaul.

In Washington, Mr. Nixon met with his Cabinet committee on international narcotics control, which is headed by Secretary of State William P. Rogers.

Violent Crimes Up in Jersey Suburbs

BY MARTIN WALDRON | NOV. 4, 1979

MATAWAN, N.J. — A report by the Federal Bureau of Investigation of an increase in crime nationally comes as no surprise to western Monmouth County. In the last year, there has been a crime explosion here, as in hundreds of New Jersey suburbs — much of it committed by juveniles, according to police officials.

Monmouth, one of the fastest growing counties in the state, has had a population gain of 30,000 since the 1970 Census. Like other South Jersey counties, Monmouth has undergone a period of rapid development, with a heavy migration from the state's more industrial northern counties.

In New Jersey's suburbs, where about three million of the state's 7.4 million residents live, violent crimes were up by more than 20 percent and nonviolent crimes up by 15 percent, while the state's cities saw increases in the two types averaging 14.7 percent.

Nationally, "serious crimes," roughly equivalent to the "violent crimes" reported in New Jersey, increased 9 percent in the first six months of the year.

MORE VANDALISM BY TEEN-AGERS

The situation has "dismayed" Governor Byrne, who has directed the state police, the major police agency in the state, to come up with a program to deal with the problem by the end of the year.

Although officials in New York and Connecticut suburbs have also expressed concern about the spread of violent crimes, only minor increases have been reported in communities around New York City. Connecticut does not break down the crime statistics by suburbs.

Suburban officials say the incidence of teen-age vandalism, arson and burglary is of particular concern.

BURGLARIES AT SCHOOLS UP

Last spring, at Keyport High School, north of here, several students said that they kept .22-caliber weapons in their school lockers and used them at lunchtime — when teachers were busy in the lunchroom — to shoot at windows and tires of cars parked in the school lots.

At Hazlet, a couple of miles east of here, suburban homes came under stone-throwing attacks that the police had thought would end with the arrest in August of a 16-year-old. But last month in Aberdeen Township, homeowners complained that houses were being hit with rocks, broken bricks and pellets from guns.

Arsonists have kept firemen busy in Keyport, with so many suspicious fires breaking out that a $1,000 reward has been posted. Among the 15 to 20 buildings burned have been nine private garages, some of them containing vehicles.

School burglaries have become so common that local school districts are installing alarm systems connected to police stations.

NASSAU REPORTS RISE IN CRIME

In interviews, almost a dozen Monmouth County officials attributed the crime "wave" to juveniles and said there appeared to have been a relaxation of parental supervision.

"We really don't know what to do about it," said Matawan's Mayor, Victor R. Armellino.

"What I would really like to see is the names of some of these juveniles published in the newspapers," Mayor Armellino said. However New Jersey prohibits this, except in unusual circumstances.

Suburbs around New York City reported some minor increases in serious crimes during the first half of this year over the same period last year. In Nassau County, the total the first six months this year was 23,109, up 1.8 percent over last year's first-half total of 22,707. The comparable figures in Suffolk County were 32,955 and 32,789; in Westchester County, 18,350 and 17,795, and in Rockland County, 4,342 and 4,647.

A spokesman for the New York Uniform Crime Reporting unit said that the Rockland figures showing a decrease were being rechecked, and that the small increases on Long Island were not considered significant.

ARRESTS OF JUVENILES INCREASE

Connecticut officials said they had begun keeping statewide crime statistics, suburban and rural. Statewide, the number of serious crimes in Connecticut — as compiled from records in almost 100 towns and cities — totaled 38,232 in the last three months of 1978. In the last three months of 1977, the total was 37,345, spokesman said.

The official position that more juveniles are committing serious crimes in New Jersey is borne out by records showing increases in arrests. The crimes included rape, robbery, atrocious assault, automobile theft, forgery and counterfeiting and disorderly conduct. In the first six months of this year there were 63,499 arrests, compared with 61,916 in the same period last year.

Much of the increase in suburban crime is believed by officials to be related to illegal drugs. About 10 percent of the more than 300,000 yearly arrests in New Jersey are for possession or sale of marijuana, cocaine or other illegal drugs.

State police attributed the increase in theft and robberies to increased mobility. In a recent analysis, they said that New Jersey's highway system, the state's compact size and the population density — greatest in the nation — made suburbs readily accessible and vulnerable.

CHAPTER 4

The 1980s and 1990s

The introduction of crack cocaine in the mid-1980s and an overall increase in handgun ownership led to a dramatic increase in property crimes and gun-related deaths. The 1990s brought date rape drugs, the first public claims of sexual harassment, and the internet, which extended the reach of sexual and other predators by giving them access to the young, the naive and the vulnerable. Crime rates peaked during this time. However, larger police forces, a drop in crack use, and other factors caused crime to begin dropping off in the late 1990s.

Citizens' Gun Use on Rise in Houston

BY THE NEW YORK TIMES | NOV. 21, 1982

HOUSTON, NOV. 20 — Tommie Phillips conceded that he was "pretty nervous" when he pointed his 20-gauge shotgun at the tall man in black gloves who had pried open the back door of his trailer home.

But Mr. Phillips, a gray-haired, 46-year-old truck driver, said he did not hesitate to shoot and kill when the man reached for a pistol. "Naturally, you can't feel good about killing somebody," Mr. Phillips recalled. "But I kept getting burglarized. I figured it was just time to take my stand."

Mr. Phillips's case was routinely referred to a grand jury, which has yet to consider the matter but is not expected to bring any charges.

While the case might be considered an uncommon occurrence in some cities, it is hardly uncommon in Houston.

Spurred in part by a soaring crime rate and by frontier attitudes toward guns, an unusually high number of residents and small-business owners in Houston are turning to deadly force to protect themselves and their property. Last year, residents of this city shot and killed 25 criminal suspects. So far this year they have fatally shot 17 other suspects. All the cases were termed justifiable homicides.

DALLAS FIGURES COMPARED

The numbers are as high in some other Texas cities. In Dallas, police officials said their most recent figures showed that residents of that city shot and killed 13 suspects last year in self-defense or in defense of their property.

"I think there's a sort of gun mentality in this state," said Capt. Grant Lappin of the Dallas Police Department. "A lot of people feel they're still responsible to a great extent for taking care of their own property and business, and that, frankly, it's their right to use their handguns to defend that property."

Captain Lappin, like police officials in Houston, said he doubted that there was any significant increase in such shootings, other than those attributable to population increases. But the shootings are noticeably more frequent in Houston and Dallas than in most large cities. In Los Angeles, police officials estimated that citizens there shoot and kill only six to eight suspects a year.

In New York, which has a population four times that of Houston and seven times that of Dallas, police officials said citizens fatally shot 15 suspects last year and six in the first six months of this year. Unlike the Houston and Dallas figures, though, the New York numbers include killings by private security guards.

MANY UNDAUNTED BY RISK

Houston police officials said that about half the shootings of citizens in this city involved confrontations between homeowners and burglary suspects and the other half involved small-business owners or their employees and suspects in robberies. None of the homeowners, business owners or employees involved in the confrontations were injured, but the police said there was an alarming increase in the number of robbery victims being slain.

"We generally advise pretty strongly against confronting robbers," Police Capt. L.N. Zoch said. "It's just too risky." Many residents here seem undaunted by the risk. In one highly publicized case, a 72-year-old man sat quietly one night earlier this year while two men held him at gunpoint after breaking into his home. When the two men turned away, the burglary victim reached under the couch, pulled out a gun and began firing, killing one of the men and wounding the other.

"I really wasn't worried, but my wife was scared to death," the man, Dan Faulwell, recalled. "And she wasn't even in the same room."

The police and prosecutors in Houston said the city's rising crime rate was a key factor in the shootings by citizens. Police officials reported that Houston's crime rate rose 17.7 percent in the first six months of this year, the highest increase for any city in the nation.

'CRIME'S ON EVERYBODY'S MIND'

"Let's face it, crime's on everybody's mind," District Attorney John B. Holmes of Houston said. Contending that many residents had become "almost obsessed" over how they could protect themselves through the use of guns, he said his office now distributed a free handbook on Texas weapons and self-defense laws.

Under Texas law, people are essentially permitted to use force or deadly force to protect both life and property if there is no other reasonable way to do so. Mr. Holmes said that to his knowledge, no Houston resident who maintained that he shot a suspect in self-defense or defense of property had been indicted in years.

To buy a gun in Texas, residents need only to be 21 years old, have a driver's license and sign a form saying they are not convicted felons or drug addicts. Unlike some other states, Texas does not require its citizens to register pistols or have a license to possess them.

Moreover, Texas officials have shown little interest in tightening the gun laws. But there has been some opposition, mainly from a handful of civil liberties advocates who contend that the gun laws are lax and the high number of citizen shootings are appalling.

"I think that in Texas, property rights are more important than civil rights," said Sandy Rabinowitz, director of the Houston chapter of the American Civil Liberties Union. She said that although she recognized a citizen's right to protect his life and property, many people were "going overboard."

"There's a kind of vigilantism that is implicitly allowed because the laws are too weak and because the D.A.'s don't prosecute," Miss Rabinowitz said.

Troubled Farmers: Debts and Guns

BY ANDREW H. MALCOLM | DEC. 12, 1985

A FINANCIALLY troubled farmer who walked into his small town bank near here Monday and shot the bank president dead had no problem driving off again into the blowing snow: The Hills Bank and Trust Company, with more than $200 million in assets, had no security guard.

In an age when body searches have become routine for airplane passengers, even children, it may seem strange that a financial institution like the Hills bank could remain largely unprotected. But it stands unguarded no longer.

One of the first official steps after the shooting was to dispatch police officers and guards to banks in the surrounding rural areas, to guard not against robbers but against disgruntled debtors. It represented the shattering of one more link in a long local chain of social trust running back for generations.

In 1983, when Rudolph H. Blythe Jr., a bank president in Ruthton, Minn., was ambushed and killed, some suggested it was an isolated incident. But as the nation's agricultural financial crisis continues into its fourth year with record numbers of farmers, banks and local businesses failing and no end in sight, there continue to be violent outbreaks and many more nonfatal incidents and threats.

TROUBLES EVERYWHERE

The current farm convulsions are the latest in a fundamental economic restructuring across the country's midsection, which historically has produced so much of the nation's foods and factories, its leaders and social values. For a complex variety of reasons, all the basic industries, the ones that produced generations of guaranteed overtime and a better life for every hard-working father's hard-working son, are in trouble across the Middle West: steel, rubber, mining, automobiles. Now comes farming, which has seen its ranks shrivel from 6.6 million farms a half century ago to 2.4 million today, 63 percent of whom are small producers.

The factory workers may resent being forced to undergo job retraining. But losing land and machinery means life retraining for an independent, middle-aged farmer who, despite years of 16-hour days, must acknowledge that he has failed to carry on his family's farm legacy.

A bank manager, too, may feel angry frustration at having to warn even reliable debtors of late payment penalties, or having to summon a lifelong friend, and announce the end of his friend's farm livelihood.

FEAR AND HELPLESSNESS

In hundreds of conversations in recent years, across the rural Middle West, both farmers and bankers said that much of this fear and frustration, this stress and sense of powerlessness, seems to come from decisions made so far away: interest rates, crop prices, grain embargoes and even foreclosures by government agencies or by the main office of a local bank recently consumed by a merger.

Small towns may never have been as idyllic as Hollywood found them, nor as venal as Sinclair Lewis described them. For some, small towns produced claustrophobia, everyone knowing everything about everyone. But for many others they produced security, creating a rational, predictable system of social values and behavior.

These rules — always appear honest, don't be nosy or pushy; in short, don't get too big for your britches — were also predictably enforced through rumors or ostracism.

Where handshakes and first names were once adequate social cement, now documents are required by distant bureaucrats or local authorities who fear the distant bureaucrats. Once a local customer's overdrawn check was likely to be overlooked by a bank officer, a friend who knew the farmer would have the money tomorrow when he sold his corn; now the check is likely to draw a computerized red flag and the attention of a young officer transferred to the little bank for two years.

Shortly before that elderly farmer in Hills shot the bank president, a teller rejected a check on his overdrawn account.

Last year the Iowa Legislature passed a law enabling any credit institution to send a list of its debtors to grain elevators and cattle sales barns, any institution where a farmer might generate money by selling his products. The law enabled banks to require these institutions to make checks payable to both the farmer and the bank.

This prohibits a few farmers from receiving income without applying at least some toward their outstanding debts, debts that in the aggregate were threatening to drown creditors in red ink. Other borrowers do pay for bad loans in the long run, and a small bank is, after all, a business whose owners are entitled to get back the money that they lend, with a profit.

But the list also suggests to many honest customers, who now have to take every check to the bank for approval just to deposit it, that they were no longer trusted, a further fraying of the social fabric. The old attitude of expecting the best from a neighbor is turning to suspecting the worst.

Such precautions also fed fears on both sides of the credit crunch, especially at bill-paying time in the fall and early winter. A recent survey of 155 Iowa agricultural bankers found 45 percent of the respondents, up from 24 percent last year, characterized relations with farmers as tense. Half the bankers said they had been verbally abused, 13 percent had been physically threatened and 4 percent were actually attacked. Some bankers admit carrying guns at times.

PSYCHOLOGICAL ISOLATION

The traditional code of the countryside requires silence outside the family on personal problems: Don't wash dirty laundry in public. In private and public sessions, mental health counselors are trying to break those taboos and build networks of neighbors for emotional support to combat the psychological isolation of depression, especially among rural males.

Jumping out a window was the answer for some financially failing stockbrokers in the Great Depression. Jumping out the window of a typical Iowa farmhouse would produce a fall of perhaps five feet. So some have reached for a rifle or shotgun, those long-familiar weapons that in many rural households outnumber the humans. And they have lashed out like lightning at the nearest target, a wife, a bank president, a farm animal or in many cases, themselves.

Much attention is lavished on the politics of the farm problem, noted an editorial in The Iowa City Press-Citizen on Tuesday. "But if there's one thing that is clear from Monday's tragic series of murder and suicide, it is that the farm crisis is not numbers and deficits and bushels of corn. It is people and pride and tears and blood."

A New, Purified Form of Cocaine Causes Alarm as Abuse Increases

BY JANE GROSS | NOV. 29, 1985

A NEW FORM of cocaine is for sale on the streets of New York, alarming law-enforcement officials and rehabilitation experts because of its tendency to accelerate abuse of the drug, particularly among adolescents.

The substance, known as crack, is already processed into the purified form that enables cocaine users to smoke, or free-base, the powerful stimulant of the central nervous system.

Previously, free-basers had to reduce cocaine powder themselves to its unadulterated form by combining it with baking soda or ether and evaporating the resulting paste over a flame.

Since crack appeared on the streets of the Bronx last year, spreading throughout the city and its suburbs, new cocaine users have graduated more quickly from inhaling to free-basing, the most addictive form of cocaine abuse.

In addition, dealers in crack have found a ready market in people reluctant to intensify their intake by intravenous injection of cocaine because of the fear of AIDS, or acquired immune deficiency syndrome, a fatal affliction that is spread by contaminated needles.

'WAVE OF THE FUTURE'

"Drug abusers are always looking for the ultimate high, asking each other, 'Did you try this, did you try that?' " said William Hopkins, a retired police officer who directs the street-research unit of the State Division of Substance Abuse Services.

"There's always something new developing, new substances, new ways of using substances. Some of things you hear of die down, but this, I have every reason to believe, is building. This is the wave of the future."

As the use of crack has increased, Federal drug officials have begun raiding "factories" where the cocaine powder is processed into pure beige crystals known as "rocks" and then packed into transparent vials resembling large vitamin capsules.

Meanwhile, narcotics officers of the New York City Police Department have shut down a few of the so-called crack houses, the rough equivalent of heroin-shooting galleries, where sales are made and users gather for smoking binges that can last for several days.

Two of the crack houses, also known as base houses, were raided recently in the Tremont section of the Bronx, according to Lieut. John Creegan, one of them in an apartment and the other in a rooming house.

"I talked to one of the women there," Lieutenant Creegan said, "and it was almost like her mind was burned out. She told me all she does is do crack all day."

Earlier this month, in what is believed to be one of the country's first raids of a crack factory, local agents of the Federal Drug Enforcement Administration arrested a cocaine dealer and then raided a Harlem apartment where he was reputedly producing 2.2 pounds of crack each day, for net daily profits of $500,000.

BUSINESS-CARD SLOGANS

In the raid, according to a D.E.A. spokesman, Andrew Fenrich, the agents seized half a pound of cocaine powder, vials of crack, six weapons, four two-way radios, scales and processing equipment, bulletproof vests and business cards embossed with slogans like "Crack It Up" and "Buy One, Get One Free."

While law-enforcement officials are increasingly turning their attention to the manufacture and sale of crack, its abusers are showing up in local treatment centers, where cocaine-related admissions were rising dramatically even before the new form of the drug was available.

Experts estimate that there are at least five million regular cocaine users in the United States, with perhaps a million of them in the metropolitan region.

According to data collected through the national cocaine hot line, (800) COCAINE, 60 percent of the users snort the drug, with the remaining 40 percent evenly divided between free-basing and intravenous use. That pattern, however, seems to be changing.

Of the three methods of use, free-basing offers the most immediate high (within 10 seconds) and the shortest one (approximately 5 minutes) and thus leads to the most frequent, debilitating and costly habit, experts say.

QUICKER GRATIFICATION

"Unlike normal cocaine, people who free-base can't stop," said Mr. Hopkins. "They free-base until all their money is used up. The way crack is spreading is almost verification of that. It pays as a distributor to free-base it, because it makes you sell your brand quicker than somebody else."

"It's a new, improved product," said Dr. Arnold M. Washton, the director of addiction research and treatment at Regent Hospital on East 61st Street in Manhattan and Stony Lodge Hospital in Ossining, N.Y. "No mess, no bother, no delay — and addicts have never been any good at delayed gratification."

Buying crack is safer than making it and often cheaper. A kit of free-base equipment — beaker, bunsen burner and pipe — costs about $14 and the chemicals are volatile, sometimes causing explosions like the one that injured the comedian Richard Pryor in 1980.

The crack sold on the street in New York ranges in cost from $2 to $50 depending on the number of rocks in the vial and, paradoxically, is sometimes less expensive than the amount of powder, currently retailing at $75 to $100 a gram, necessary to produce the equivalent free-base.

CRACKING IMAGINARY WHIP

Experts assume that crack deals are also being made in the suburbs, although less conspicuously than in New York, where Mr. Hopkins's street researchers, all of them former addicts, describe dealers standing on street corners cracking an imaginary whip to signal their wares. "In middle-class neighborhoods," Mr. Hopkins said, "it's handled differently — indoors."

Dr. Washton, who is also the research director for the cocaine hot line, predicts an "epidemic" of free-basing because of the availability of crack, and he is gathering demographic data on its use from a sample of recent callers. After examining information from the first 100 callers in his survey, Dr. Washton reported that 27 of them had used crack and found it easy to purchase, and that the crack users averaged 17 years of age.

Dr. Washton first heard about crack early this year from two 17-year-old patients at Stony Lodge, the suburban psychiatric hospital. Both youths reported that they had snorted cocaine for a while, but did not become compulsive until they tried crack — doubling, tripling and quadrupling their use, missing school, stealing from their parents and lying to their friends.

A VULNERABLE POPULATION

"These were kids from upper-middle-class families in Scarsdale and Mamaroneck," Dr. Washton said, "kids with no history of addiction or psychiatric illness. They were in the top half of their class, college bound, and they were addicted almost instantaneously. They were rendered completely dysfunctional by crack in a two- or three-month period."

"The most vulnerable population is adolescents," agreed Kevin McEneaney, the director of clinical services at Phoenix House, an international network of rehabitative centers. "Kids will overconsume and burn themselves out, fizzle, very quickly."

Mr. McEneaney also said he was concerned by reports of sexual degradation from women using crack. Cocaine, particularly in its free-base form, is a euphoriant and its users often describe increased sexual appetite and an interest in previously untried sexual practices.

According to Mr McEneaney, patients have told him that crack houses are the scene of "uncontrollable, outrageous" sexual activity, with women frequently exchanging sex for drugs when they have run out of money.

"The behavioral stuff we're hearing about," Mr. McEneaney said, "drives home that what we're dealing with, and not in the physical sense, is the most powerful drug we've ever seen. These women wake up one day and they cannot believe the degrading and bizarre things they've been involved with."

MEDICAL COMPLICATIONS

Finally, Mr. McEneaney said, there is the risk of unpredictable medical complications. By stimulating the central nervous system — increasing heart and respiration rates and elevating blood pressure and body temperature — cocaine has been known to cause coronary arrest, strokes, convulsive seizures and other less serious disorders.

"No one knows what happens to people who blow themselves out for days," Mr. McEneaney said. "The toll to be paid in the future could be profound. It's impossible to think people can do the things we're talking about without sustaining physiological damage."

"Yes, it increases the danger of toxic and overdose reactions," Dr. Washton said. "But the biggest danger, because admittedly most people won't die, is the overwhelming compulsion to repeat the experience."

The medical experts and law-enforcement officials agree that crack should not be considered merely a slight variation of the cocaine that is snorted because free-basing is such a different experience, both qualitatively and quantitatively.

"The high these people describe is not even comparable," Dr. Washton said. "It is unmatched in its euphoria and exhilaration. Clinicians need to know about it. Parents need to know about it. Law-enforcement people in other parts of the country need to know about it. In no way should it be compared to snorting cocaine hydrochloride powder. It's almost like we're talking about a different drug here."

A Rising Tide of Violence Leaves More Youths in Jail

BY SUSAN DIESENHOUSE | JULY 8, 1990

A RISING NUMBER of the country's adolescents are being arrested for violent crimes, with a record 100,000 of them confined in correctional institutions on any given day. Although the number of young people is declining as the country's population ages, experts say an increase in poverty, drug use and single-parent families is feeding the problem and compelling states to re-examine juvenile justice programs.

With the second baby boom — the baby boomers' babies — coming of age, the adolescent population is expected to grow in the next decade. The cost of maintaining or expanding jails is already taxing government resources, forcing many states to ask how they are going to weather what many fear will be a rising wave of violent crime. Should they follow states like New York, California, Florida, Arizona and South Carolina, which favor tough policies on detention? Or should they try the rehabilitative approach, pioneered by Massachusetts in the 1970's and later by Utah, which stresses a mix of punishment, restitution and social services?

While there are many shades between the extremes, most states, by far, follow the "get tough" approach advocated for years by the Reagan and Bush administrations. Attorney General Dick Thornburgh summed up the stance in a speech in May when he said that violent youthful offenders should be tried as adults and given the same sentences, including the death penalty.

But with the penal system strained to the breaking point, many states are considering other approaches. Florida, Oregon, California, Oklahoma, Maryland and the District of Columbia are facing court orders to upgrade their systems. Others, such as Missouri, Hawaii,

Louisiana, Idaho, Tennessee, Virginia, Colorado, Delaware and Michigan are experimenting with innovative programs, according to the Center for Youth Policy, a study group at the University of Michigan.

Recently Florida began moving away from its strict policy, under which 5,000 juveniles were brought before adult courts in 1989. The state is embarking on a $150 million, two-year program to set up community-based rehabilitation programs. "The past approach was ineffective, expensive and manufactured youthful criminals," said Albert J. Hadeed, special counsel to the Speaker of the Florida state legislature, who supported the changes.

In Massachusetts, few young criminals are jailed. Although 1,700 juveniles were committed to the system last year, only about 170 spaces were available in lockup. Most offenders are placed in professionally staffed community homes or kept under supervision while they make restitution for their crimes, get treatment and training and maintain ties with family, school and community. The state can point to a comparatively low recidivism rate. Only 23 percent of the juveniles released from the program were recommitted within three years and the state, which ranks 46th in juvenile crime, has not seen as steep a rise in youth violence as many other states, according to the National Council on Crime and Delinquency, a nonprofit group in San Francisco.

California, where the juvenile incarceration rate is 566 per 100,000, compared with a national average of 244 and the Massachusetts rate of 133, has a recommittment rate of 62 percent and had a 10 percent rise in the juvenile crime rate in 1989.

But Massachusetts has not gone unscathed and it is under pressure to take a tougher approach, said Edward J. Loughran, the Commissioner of the Department of Youth Services, which is in charge of the juvenile correction system. William R. Celester, the deputy superintendent of the Boston Police Department, said, "We have never had the violence among young people we are experiencing today."

Bills before the Massachusetts legislature would allow judges to sentence young offenders to juvenile detention centers or adult prisons.

"If it is a serious crime, no matter the age of the offenders, they should do serious time in many circumstances," said Karen A. McLaughlin, director of the state's Office for Victim Assistance.

But Jerome G. Miller, director of the National Center on Institutions and Alternatives and the former juvenile corrections commissioner who instituted the Massachusetts system, said, "A very decent system that shows how well a state can do without locking up huge numbers is about to be jettisoned."

Nationally since 1975, murders committed by juveniles have increased three times, rapes two times and robberies five times, said Robert W. Sweet Jr., the Administrator of the United States Department of Justice's Juvenile Justice and Delinquency Prevention Program.

In 1989, the House Committee on Children, Youth and Families reported a "national emergency" of growing violence by and against youth, with homicide becoming the leading killer of black males aged 15 to 24 and the second cause for whites after car accidents. Each day about 100,000 juveniles are held in custody, according to the National Council on Crime and Delinquency. About 92,000 are in juvenile institutions, the rest in adult prisons. In 1979 the number in juvenile institutions was about 72,000.

Most experts agree that the violence reflects a breakdown of families, schools and other community institutions. Combine that with increasing high school dropout rates, more teen pregnancies, and more drug use and health and nutritional deficiencies and the nation's future is in "Code Blue," a state of medical emergency, said a recent report by the American Medical Association and the State Boards of Education. According to the report, about 20 percent of the country's children grow up in poverty, a 50 percent increase since 1969.

Against this backdrop, officials in Washington are debating what role the Federal Government should play in fighting juvenile crime.

"Federal Government can never stop these problems," said Mr. Sweet, the Justice Department official. "There is a general breakdown of the primary defenders against juvenile delinquency at the local level."

But Representative George Miller, the California Democrat who is chairman of the Select Committee on Children, said the Federal Government has abdicated its responsibility by cutting domestic programs. "For the poor, violence has become a survival skill," he said.

The committee reported that from 1981 to 1987 Federal cuts, adjusted for inflation, decreased support for child welfare services by 32 percent, for alcohol, drug and mental health treatment by 30 percent, for food stamps and other safety net programs for poor families by 72 percent, for college grants by 38.6 percent and for juvenile delinquency prevention by 55 percent.

Mr. Celester, the Boston police official, said, "Youth violence is rising because the problems that cause it aren't being addressed: lack of education or training for jobs with a future, housing, recreational facilities, drug treatment on demand."

Senate Votes Sweeping Crime Bill, Banning Some Assault Weapons

BY STEVEN A. HOLMES | JULY 12, 1990

THE SENATE TODAY overwhemingly approved a crime bill that includes a temporary ban on the sale and manufacture of certain semiautomatic assault weapons, greater Federal assistance to law-enforcement agencies and an expansion of the number of Federal crimes for which the death penalty can be imposed.

The Senate passed the crime bill after voting to include an amendment that would provide $162 million to combat fraud in the savings and loan industry. The total cost of the crime package would be about $2 billion a year.

'THE TOUGHEST CRIME BILL'

The measure, the Omnibus Crime Bill, passed by a vote of 94 to 6, with four of the opponents voting against it because of their opposition to capital punishment.

"This is the toughest, most comprehensive crime bill in our history," said Senator Joseph R. Biden Jr., the Democrat from Delaware who was the measure's chief sponsor.

The action by the Senate, which came after months of political wrangling and behind-the-scenes negotiations, shifts the crime issue to the House, where a number of anti-crime measures are pending. Speaker Thomas S. Foley of Washington has vowed that the House will consider these bills, either separately or as part of a crime package, before the next recess, which begins on Aug. 6.

The prospects for House passage of an anti-crime measure appear good. It is unclear, however, whether any gun control legislation will be approved.

The Senate bill expanded to 34 from 23 the number of Federal crimes that would warrant the death penalty. In addition to treason, espionage and the assassination of the President, capital crimes would include kidnapping, the taking of a hostage, the killing of a foreign official and murdering for money.

The bill would also limit, in most cases, death row inmates sentenced under state law to one appeal of their sentence on constitutional grounds in Federal courts, and it would add 2,500 Federal law-enforcement agents.

In addition, the legislation would set up a scholarship program for college students who agree to serve as police officers for four years after graduation, and would provide $900 million in aid to state and local law-enforcement agencies — twice the amount President Bush had asked for.

BUSH SUPPORTS THE MEASURE

A White House spokesman said today that President Bush supported the Senate bill, despite its three-year ban on nine types of semiautomatic pistols, rifles and shotguns — a ban the President opposes. "Our position on the semiautomatic weapons ban is well known," said the spokesman, Alixe Glen. "But overall, we feel the package is a good one."

Ms. Glen said, however, that the Administration "has a couple of problems" with a House version that would permanently bar the sale, manufacture or possession of a larger number of semiautomatic weapons and impose a seven-day waiting period for an individual who tried to buy a firearm.

The bill passed today by the Senate had been stalled since May 23 when gun control opponents fell one vote short of defeating the amendment by Senator Dennis DeConcini, an Arizona Democrat, that imposed the ban on some semiautomatic weapons. While the weapons provision was the most divisive, in the end, four of the Senators who voted against the bill did so because they oppose capital punishment. They were Senators Edward M. Kennedy of Massachusetts and Howard M. Metzenbaum of Ohio, both Democrats, and Mark O. Hatfield of Oregon and Dave Durenberger of Minnesota, Republicans.

The other two Senators who voted against the bill were William V. Roth of Delaware and William I. Armstrong of Colorado, both Republicans. Mr. Armstrong objected, in part, to the ban on semiautomatic weapons. Mr. Roth thought the measure was too costly.

The Senate bill bans for three years the import or domestic manufacture of nine types of semiautomatic weapons encompassing 14 models. These include the Kalashnikov, the Uzi and Galil, the Beretta AR-70, the Colt AR-15 and CAR-15, the MAC-10 and MAC-11, the Inratec TEC-9 and the Street Sweeper, a semi-automatic shotgun developed in South Africa.

Gun control advocates cheered passage of the crime bill, saying that it indicated the waning influence of the National Rifle Association.

"I think it provides big momentum for us," said Sarah Brady, chairman of Handgun Control Inc., whose husband, James Brady, was severely wounded by an assassin's bullet meant for President Ronald Reagan. "I think it just shows tremendously how the tide has turned in this country and that the word has gotten to the U.S. Congress. They want to put an end to the violence."

In the House, the Judiciary Committee has approved a more stringent ban that would permanently bar the sale, manufacture and possession of a larger number of semiautomatic weapons. That committee is also scheduled to consider a bill that would impose a seven-day waiting period for anyone seeking to purchase a firearm.

In recent years, the House has been more pro-gun control than the Senate. But unlike the Senate, all members of the House are up for re-election this year and it is expected that the National Rifle Association will apply intense pressure in an effort to kill any gun control measure in the House.

"The N.R.A. really has incentive to put on big-time full court press over there on assault weapons," said a Senate aide involved in the issue. "That makes the House a real question mark."

Gun control opponents appear nervous about what President Bush would do should the Senate bill emerge from a House-Senate conference.

"I think it's up in the air what Bush would do," said Wayne LaPierre, executive director of the N.R.A.'s Institute of Legislative Action. "We are sure he would rather it didn't end up on his desk in terms of the gun provisions."

Two years ago, Congress approved the death penalty for major narcotics traffickers who commit murder. The Senate bill passed today contains an amendment sponsored by Senator Alfonse M. D'Amato, Republican of New York, providing the death penalty for major narcotics dealers involved in drug conspiracies.

There have been no executions for Federal crimes since 1972 when the Supreme Court ruled that the Federal Government and states had to establish procedures to allow juries to consider aggravating and mitigating circumstances of a crime before sentencing a defendant to death. The Senate bill sets up those procedures.

The legislation also allows tribal councils on Indian reservations to determine if a person can be executed for committing a crime on tribal land. Because the Federal crimes for which the capital punishment can be imposed occur so seldom, it is unlikely that the Senate bill, should it become law, would lead to a surge in executions. "It is vastly overblown in terms of significance," said Mr. Biden of the bill's death penalty provisions.

BILL WOULD LIMIT APPEALS

Far more significant is the section limiting, with some exceptions, state death row inmates to one appeal in Federal courts of the constitutionality of their sentences. The provision would apply only in states that provide death row inmates with free, competent legal counsel to help them prepare their appeals. Currently, condemned prisoners have an unlimited number of appeals. Critics of the system note that it takes an average of eight years from the time a defendant is sentenced to die and the time the sentence is carried out.

The bill would also add a total of 2,500 new agents to the Federal Bureau of Investigation, the Drug Enforcement Agency and the Customs Service. It also imposes new penalties for possession and sale of "ice," a potent, smokable form of methamphetamines.

Asked whether Congress would vote to appropriate the total amount of money budgeted under the bill, Mr. Biden said, "We will get the money."

Pregnant, Addicted — and Guilty?

BY JAN HOFFMAN | AUG. 19, 1990

TRAVELING WEST from Detroit about 200 miles along I-96, crack arrived in Muskegon County, Mich., late in September 1988. Or at least that's when the prosecutor Tony Tague first started noticing that a crime rampage was rocking this hard-scrabble, blue-collar county — the kind of siege that supposedly strikes only the nation's largest cities. With only 161,000 people scattered across 7 cities and 16 townships, Muskegon County, a scenic but tired factory area with an unemployment rate nearly double the national average, would appear to be scarcely worth the picking. "The Detroit drug dealers told us that Muskegon is such a welfare town that it's guaranteed income for them when the checks come in," recalls Detective Sgt. Al Van Hemert, a ruddy veteran narcotics cop.

Muskegon's murders, break-ins and muggings began to rise dramatically. District judges were spending three days a week instead of one on drug cases, and the county jail became dangerously overcrowded. A special 72-CRACK phone line rang constantly. Tague, the 32-year-old son of a retired local police chief, conducted a high-profile antidrug crusade, but his office simply became overwhelmed.

A year after crack hit the area, county social workers removed 27 children in just one month from crack-afflicted homes. Three of the children belonged to a 23-year-old black single mother named Kimberly Ann Hardy. Hardy came to the attention of the county's Department of Social Services because she was the first woman reported by Muskegon General Hospital to bear a child who tested positive for crack cocaine.

It was time, concluded Tony Tague, to send a message. Choosing a controversial new tactic already employed by prosecutors in Florida, Georgia, South Carolina and Massachusetts, Tague ordered Kimberly Hardy arrested on the same charge prosecutors routinely use against drug dealers: delivering drugs in the amount of less than 50 grams, a felony in Michigan carrying a mandatory minimum jail term of one year and a maximum of 20 years.

To avoid becoming embroiled in debates over when the fetus becomes a person, the prosecutor contended that Hardy delivered crack to her son through her umbilical cord during the 90 seconds or so after the child had left the birth canal but before the cord was cut.

Almost from the outset, Tague maintained that his objective was not to send women to prison, but to protect children. As Sergeant Van Hemert says: "We want to avoid becoming a Detroit or a New York. Our attitude is, 'Hey, let's stop it now!' It's a form of caring."

Crack babies seem to be everywhere, and they will not go away. Cautionary images of shrieking infants, bug-eyed as if they are watching tape loops from hell, even march across public-service announcements during televised sports events. A frequently cited nationwide study claimed that last year, 375,000 children may have been affected by their mother's drug use during pregnancy. Strokes in utero and respiratory and neurological disorders are only a few of the most common problems plaguing these drastically underweight children.

Their suffering, to say nothing of the long-term social costs, is so staggering that people understandably want to turn on their perceived torturers: their mothers. "If the mother wants to smoke crack and kill herself, I don't care," Sergeant Van Hemert says flatly. "Let her die, but don't take that poor baby with her." In a 15-state survey by The Atlanta Constitution, 71 percent of the 1,500 people polled favored criminal penalties for pregnant women whose drug use injured their babies.

At their recent conventions, the National District Attorneys Association and the American Bar Association took up the national debate about law enforcement's increasingly aggressive role in penalizing these women: should the threat of criminal prosecution be used to drive them toward treatment? Michael Barber, the Sacramento attorney who was chairman of the A.B.A.'s family-law section this year, favors discretionary criminal sanctions, such as supervised probation, as well as "threatened incarceration if, when she's pregnant, she's still taking drugs." Although many legal experts prefer that these cases remain in family courts, which can order treatment and removal of children but not jail sentences, Barber is dubious. "Family courts don't provide the control factor in the mother that we need to prevent the repetition of this activity," he says.

In the last few years, more and more judges and lawmakers have come to view these mothers as criminals who victimize children, rather than as victims themselves. Since 1987, 19 states and the District of Columbia have instigated more than 50 criminal proceedings against mothers for drug abuse during their pregnancies, according to the American Civil Liberties Union, which has vigorously opposed these measures. (With the exception of a few cases, prosecutors have not gone after pregnant alcoholics. In many states, giving alcohol to a minor is only a misdemeanor.) Last summer, Jennifer Johnson of Florida became the first woman in the country to be convicted of making a drug delivery to her baby; she was sentenced to 14 years on probation. Most prosecutors concede that widespread prison terms for pregnant mothers are not feasible. But in May, a Kentucky woman who gave birth to three children during her 17-year addiction to pills and intravenous drugs was sentenced to five years in prison for criminal child abuse. In North Carolina a few months ago, a prosecutor charged an addicted mother whose newborn had a positive toxicology test with a more pernicious crime — assault with a deadly weapon.

"The war on drugs has degenerated into a war on women," says Alan S. Rapoport, Kim Hardy's attorney. "And why is it that all these straight white men are telling pregnant women how they should act and feel?"

Feminists and civil libertarians argue that prosecuting women for what is in essence their conduct during pregnancy abrogates constitutional rights to privacy and turns pregnant users into second-class citizens, deprived of equal protection. They also invoke the "slippery slope" argument — if the line isn't drawn at drug abuse, will prosecutors go after pregnant women for drinking, smoking or even taking aspirin?

Prosecutors maintain that they are simply protecting children. But defense attorneys retort that law-enforcement officials are forcing a wedge between mother and child, making the relationship adversarial — "fetal rights" versus "maternal rights." Their interests should instead be seen as joined, argued a recent Harvard Law Review article on state intervention during pregnancy. "The harm to the fetus does not make the woman's addiction more criminal. Rather, it highlights the severity of her disease."

But at least eight states now include drug exposure in utero in their definition of child abuse and neglect — and many more have legislation pending. Some states and many local jurisdictions require nothing but a positive drug test to remove an infant from a mother. Dr. Ira J. Chasnoff, who supplied an affidavit supporting Hardy, says that penalties against addicted mothers tend to fall much more heavily on poor minority women. As an example, Dr. Chasnoff, the founder and president of the National Association of Perinatal Addiction Research and Education, points to Florida's Pinellas County, where pregnant black users are nearly 10 times more likely to be reported for substance abuse than pregnant white users. Treatment programs for pregnant addicts are scarce enough, he warns; prosecutions only scare addicts away from seeking even basic prenatal care, for fear they'll be turned in.

Dr. Chasnoff doesn't have much regard for the legal theory that cocaine is passed through the umbilical cord just before it's clamped. "Good ethics and good law have to be based on good science," he says, "and we just don't have that kind of data."

State courts have been divided over whether indicting pregnant addicts is within the scope of existing drug-delivery statutes. Michigan is now considering the question. On June 2, a few days before Hardy was to go on trial, the Michigan Court of Appeals, in a highly unusual move, elected to hear arguments about whether her case should be tried in the lower circuit court or be thrown out altogether. A decision will probably not be reached until early this fall. The outcome of the Hardy case, which is being eagerly awaited across the country by law-enforcement officials, civil libertarians and feminists, as well as health-care officials, may help determine whether the door to future prosecutions will be open or closed, But with the exception of Hardy herself, perhaps no one is awaiting the decision more eagerly than a 36-year-old attorney and single mother named Lynn Ellen Bremer. On July 18, Bremer, who is white, became the second woman in Muskegon County to be bound over for trial on charges of drug delivery to her infant.

Kim Hardy smoked crack the night before she gave birth to her son, Areanis, on Aug. 20, 1989, as she freely admitted to Sergeant Van Hemert. Lynn Bremer told him that 40 hours before her daughter, Brittany, was born on April 10 of this year, she snorted a gram of cocaine with some friends to celebrate her birthday.

The prosecution developed its case against each woman in similar fashion. It began with drug tests, performed during labor. Hardy's urine had been screened for drugs shortly after she showed up at Muskegon General. According to a policy adopted by many public hospitals, Hardy qualified as a "high- risk pregnancy" — she'd had no prenatal care and was six to eight weeks early. At Hackley Hospital, Bremer's own obstetrician ordered her tested because he had known about her cocaine addiction for nearly five months. Despite his threats to drop her as a patient if she didn't stop using, she had refused both residential and outpatient treatment.

But neither woman was asked to sign an informed consent for the screens on herself or her child — which defense attorneys across the country have turned into a key issue in many of these cases. Hardy's lawyers argued that the tests violated her rights to privacy and against self-incrimination. Meanwhile, the prosecution maintained that drug-testing constitutes sound medical practice and that permission could be considered to have been granted under the patient's general consent form. Bremer's daughter weighed 6 pounds and was apparently healthy. But Hardy's 5-pound son was jaundiced, constipated and could not keep down his formula; he had a small head and developed a mysterious infection. After the women were discharged, the hospitals kept the infants for observation, tested them for drugs and reported the positive results to the Department of Social Services. Both Hardy and Bremer were given 24 hours' notice to appear at emergency hearings to determine the temporary removal of their newborns. Although social workers later remarked that neither of Hardy's older children, then 4 years old and 11 months old, respectively, appeared neglected, because of the positive tests on the newborn and her admitted use, they too were immediately sent to foster care.

In despair over losing their children, Hardy and Bremer used drugs one more time. Then they entered 30-day residential treatment programs. While Tague took credit for this, both women asserted that their motive was to clean themselves up and get their children back. Tague announced to the news media that they would be arrested once their treatment had been completed.

Drug use, which both women admitted, is a rarely applied misdemeanor in Michigan that's punishable by probation — especially in a first-offense case. But because they were pregnant when they used drugs, they were charged instead with the felony of drug delivery. "Arrest pregnant women for possession or use, the same thing you'd arrest a man for," says Lynn Paltrow of the A.C.L.U. "But these women are being prosecuted for the crime of becoming pregnant while having an addiction problem."

Tague has little patience for this line of thinking: "It's easy for the defense attorneys to throw out academic arguments about why we should not be proceeding. Why aren't they concerned about the constitutional rights of the child to be born drug free?"

Judge Frederic Grimm Jr. of District Court, who had ordered Hardy to stand trial after preliminary hearings, took a narrow focus in his ruling. "I feel sympathetic toward the defendant," he said recently, "but her behavior is proscribed criminal behavior. And you don't excuse it by saying she's disadvantaged or a mother."

Shortly after the birth of her second child, Nyeassa, in the fall of 1988, Kim Hardy had started smoking crack. A friend from New York had introduced her to the new drug. In Muskegon, crack comes in miniature Ziploc plastic bags and sells for an inflated $20 a rock. "It was the 'in' thing to do in Muskegon Heights," says Hardy. "I had no sense of the danger." Soon, she was snitching her boyfriend's household money and showing up at the low-rise projects in the Heights where young dealers clustered in the parking lots.

As she recounts her story, Hardy seems older than 23. She is blunt, with a no-nonsense gravity that occasionally makes way for a tart sense of humor. "I am not a welfare mother," she says evenly. "I am on assistance." She grew up in Newton, Miss., where her three children have been living in the foster care of her parents. Her father, an auto mechanic, and mother, an industrial seamstress, used to drive the family around the country during summer vacations, which only whetted Hardy's appetite to leave town as soon as possible.

In her senior year of high school, she became pregnant, the last of her circle to do so. Abortion was not an option. Her parents were Jehovah's Witnesses, and a child, she felt, "was the one thing in the world that was mine. He was a part of me, my body." She managed to get her high-school diploma and four years ago moved with her son, Darius, to Muskegon, where she had relatives.

Muskegon is a rough place to make a fresh start, with thousands of Dutch, Polish and black workers laid off from auto-parts factories gone belly-up in recent years. She finally got a job on an assembly line at Stanco Metal Products. When she became pregnant with Nyeassa, the smell of burning oil exacerbated her nausea. She quit and went on assistance, intending to go back to work a few months after the baby was born.

Ronald Brown, her 35-year-old boyfriend, already had four children by a former wife when he met Kim. Those children, who had been exposed to drugs, alcohol and violence throughout their lives, were now scattered throughout foster-care homes and prison. One, according to the Department of Social Services, which has worked with Ronald and his family for 14 years, was born severely disabled because of the mother's drug abuse and alcoholism. Ronald himself has been in alcohol-treatment programs for years.

After the birth of Nyeassa, her daughter with Ronald, Hardy's menstrual cycle was irregular and, she recalls, it wasn't until March of last year that she realized she had probably become pregnant again — within months of delivering Nyeassa. But by then, Hardy was having a lot of domestic turmoil with Ronald. She also had a serious crack problem.

"I was in a lot of denial," she says now. "I thought I could cure myself."

Even if Hardy had been willing to consider it, residential treatment would have been almost impossible to obtain. Very few programs nationwide accept pregnant addicts, largely because of liability problems posed by high-risk pregnancies. Medicaid covers only 17 days of a typical 28-day treatment, which, given the high recidivism rate of crack users in recovery, is like "spitting in the ocean," says Barbara A. Klingenmaier, the Muskegon County foster-care supervisor.

Soon after she learned she was pregnant, Hardy, convinced she had to get away from her crowd of crack users as well as her crumbling relationship with Ronald, took the kids home to Mississippi for the duration of her pregnancy. But by moving, she lost all her welfare benefits, including Medicaid. Unable to pay for clinic visits, she had to go without prenatal care. In August, hoping to patch up things with Ronald, she returned to Muskegon to give birth. They were going to call the baby Areanis, a name they had heard on a Star Trek episode.

Even though Muskegon County is cooled by shore breezes from Lake Michigan, it can smell pretty bad in the summer, when sour fumes from the paper mill or the waste-treatment plant blow in the wrong direction. Kim Hardy had been feeling heavy and uncomfortable all that steamy day, Aug. 19. A couple of Ronald's friends showed up in the evening and woke her up, offering her crack. Maybe, she thought groggily, it would help her relax and go into labor. The baby was so far along that a couple of hits couldn't possibly hurt.

Two months ago, Tague's office sent a letter to the Department of Social Services. The letter was a strongly worded request that the agency comply with a Michigan law requiring it to notify the prosecutor whenever it found instances of child abuse. By Tague's definition, child abuse included "substantial evidence of cocaine or alcohol abuse by a woman during pregnancy." Social-service workers would now be additionally compelled to report details of the woman's addiction, as well as whether her umbilical-cord fluid had been tested. (An issue in both the Hardy and Bremer cases has been the preservation of evidence: neither umbilical cord was tested, much less saved.) The letter underscores the difficult and compromising position of the social workers, who are expected to both aid and inform on their clients. In Muskegon County, an unusual amount of interdepartmental quid pro quo is essential, because the prosecutor handles not only criminal matters but all Department of Social Services juvenile court cases as well. Social workers have to feed the prosecutor; otherwise, the cases may fall to the back of his calendar.

Vicki Birdsall, a social worker who investigated both Hardy and Bremer and alerted Sergeant Van Hemert, doesn't have misgivings about her role. She even believes that prosecution can be "therapeutic." But she thinks that drug delivery is too narrow a charge, and instead favors a statutory broadening of criminal child abuse to include fetuses. "One of my coke babies had retinal damage and seizures and to me that is just as severe as somebody whaling on a kid," she says.

But Barbara Klingenmaier, the foster-care supervisor who helped place the Bremer and Hardy children, maintains that criminal prosecution of drug-addicted mothers undercuts their fragile self-esteem and can impede recovery. She says these cases should remain under the jurisdiction of juvenile court, which has the authority to punish the mother by ordering children removed. "That is the impetus to change their behavior in most of our cases," she says.

Tony Tague seems impervious to criticism that he's crossed over the line. "We have taken progressive steps in prosecution," he says, "and as a result have been engaged in a lot of controversy. Traditional means are no longer able to address the kind of problems we're confronting. There's a real need for innovative methods."

Tague, who trained in the Manhattan District Attorney's office, is emblematic of the "Thirtysomething" generation of prosecutors — tough, of course, but also politically astute and ambitious. In putting his own imprimatur on the war on drugs, Tague has become a bona fide Muskegon celebrity whose office passes out stickers and pins that say: "Help Tony Tague Fight Drugs!"

Tague maintains that a major goal of the Bremer and Hardy prosecutions has been accomplished: the women entered treatment. Because of his campaign, he says, more and more women have become aware of the dangerous connection between drugs and pregnancy: "When physicians make suggestions, it doesn't appear that's enough for them to seek treatment. The possibility of prosecution is a strong incentive."

Sitting in her attorney's office, which, in the way of small communities, happens to be in the same building at the Muskegon mall where she and Kim Hardy's attorney practice, Lynn Bremer vehemently shakes her head. "Tony Tague is telling women to get treatment and they won't be prosecuted. I'm a perfect example of someone who tried to reach out, and it's all coming back in my face."

Adds her attorney, Norman Halbower: "You're guilty of not getting a cure soon enough."

Bremer, who is from a well-to-do local family and clerked for several Muskegon County circuit judges, finally confessed her two-year cocaine addiction to her obstetrician about four months into her pregnancy. She was estranged from her family and, despite the admonitions of her boyfriend, also a cocaine user, she felt that the doctor was the only person she could turn to. "I knew I couldn't quit," she says, "and I wanted somebody to keep a check on me."

The doctor urged her to go into a residential treatment program, but Bremer, having recently joined a law firm, did not want to jeopardize her job. Then, too, Bremer's long work days pretty much ruled out the possibility of even a four-hour-a-week outpatient program. So, instead, she saw a drug counselor for a half-dozen sessions. She did manage to cut down her use, she says, but still flunked a number of urine tests administered by her obstetrician. One time, knowing she would not pass, she even brought someone else's specimen to his office.

"I tried, I really tried, but I couldn't do it," she says, in a whispery, halting voice. "I moved out of my boyfriend's house to get away from it, and I'd go along for a while, and then some people would come over and … it just looked good."

In addition to her criminal case, Bremer, like Hardy, still faces a juvenile court case for neglecting her infant daughter, Brittany, who has been placed temporarily in foster care. Meanwhile, she has volunteered for random drug tests and warily goes for counseling. "I feel betrayed," Bremer says. "Everyone I talked to about my drug problem has been subpoenaed."

Bremer, while awaiting trial, is back at work now, but it's particularly difficult to appear as an attorney when everyone in the courtroom knows she's also a defendant. She questions whether she can get an unbiased trial in a county where she's argued cases before all the judges.

These days Bremer is living apart from her boyfriend, Jeffrey Coon, a 32-year-old assembly-line worker, who is also in recovery. "Although we're on good terms," she says, "sometimes it burns me up because he's not charged with anything, and he was right there doing it all with me. I wish he would have to do some squirming, too."

Bremer's spirits are low. "I'm embarrassed and sad," she says. "My reputation is gone, and I still don't have my daughter with me. This whole thing has turned making a baby into a tragic event."

On the last Saturday in June, hours before Muskegon's gala annual parade, Hardy is talking cheerfully about how things are finally looking up. "Life is a lot simpler now," she says with a laugh. "It's a lot cheaper without drugs." Hardy's been clean since mid-October. Social workers describe her turnaround as "extraordinary." In a few short weeks, her kids, who are reportedly in fine shape, will be returned to her after a 10-month absence. She sees a drug counselor, has made a new circle of friends and has just rented a modest three-bedroom house in a predominantly white neighborhood of Muskegon. That gives her pause, but at least it's far away from her old haunts. Besides, she is thankful that someone was willing to rent to her.

Since her case broke in the papers, she's become a public figure. She can't find a job, she says, because she is recognized as that drug mother. "Some people look at me like I'm an infection," she says.

But this fall, she starts classes in Muskegon Community College's new chemical dependency program. Noting the lack of black female counselors, Hardy says she intends to get a master's degree and become a drug therapist.

In retrospect, although she doesn't believe that she should be facing the prospect of going to jail — to say nothing of being prosecuted in the first place — Hardy is actually grateful for what's happened to her: she's stopped smoking crack. "Why is it that we have to make women criminals before we can get them drug treatment?" asks Kary Moss of the A.C.L.U.

One of Hardy's attorneys, Alan Rapoport, has an answer to Moss's question. "This crusade is not about getting women into treatment or protecting babies," he says acidly. "It's about winning the war on drugs."

Moss points out that in spite of Tony Tague's insistence that he is inspiring addicted mothers to get help, the real choice is not between prosecution and treatment, but between prosecution and virtually nothing. Most drug programs were set up to treat male heroin addicts and have no obstetrician on staff. A recent study by Dr. Wendy Chavkin of the Columbia University School of Public Health and Beth Israel Medical Center found that 87 percent of New York City's drug-abuse programs turned away pregnant crack addicts, even though the women were eligible for Medicaid. And the rare clinics that do admit them almost never have child-care facilities — a critical shortcoming for most mothers.

The effects of Tague's prosecutions are certainly being felt at the recovery-care unit at Muskegon General Hospital, which now has

11 beds for residential treatment and four for detoxification. Cheryl Gawkowski, a staff psychologist, reports that some pregnant addicts have sought help specifically because of their fear of going to jail, while others have avoided prenatal care altogether for exactly the same reason. "I go back and forth on the issue," she admits.

Hardy's opinion doesn't waver at all. A pregnant addict should be encouraged as strongly as possible to enter treatment, she says, but not forced to go. "She has to do it for herself," Hardy says. "It's a disease — just like alcoholism — and women are not going to stop until they're ready."

Only if the child is born testing positive for drugs, Hardy believes, should social services use their authority to intervene, removing the baby until the mother gets treatment. "Prosecutors don't protect babies, child protective services workers do," she says.

She doesn't know how long her own case will be hanging over her head. "It could take years. But for today, things are O.K., and I'm just looking forward to my kids coming home."

Fight Guns, Not Just Drugs

OPINION | BY THE NEW YORK TIMES | DEC. 8, 1990

THE HOMICIDE RATE for young black men has jumped by two-thirds in recent years, reaching levels in some areas that now exceed the death rate for American soldiers in Vietnam. The vast majority of those killings were committed with guns, according to a new Federal analysis. Meanwhile, murder rates for all races in New York and the District of Columbia are soaring to record levels this year, continuing a sadly predictable trend. But police in those cities add a surprising footnote: Fewer murders are drug-related. That demonstrates how much reducing urban violence requires tough policies against guns as well as drugs.

A recent weekend's violence in the nation's capital has already pushed total homicides this year past last year's record of 434. In New York City, a string of homicides last weekend brought the unofficial count to more than 2,000, also a historic high.

Police find fewer murders related to drug dealing or addiction. In Washington, such homicides account for only 39 percent of the total, compared with 52 percent last year and 66 percent in 1988. In New York, the figure for this year is 25 percent, down from 28 percent last year and 38 percent in 1980.

Increases in urban homicides appear to arise from increases in juvenile crime. Police report that schoolyard fights once settled with fists or knives now routinely escalate to shootouts. Two of New York City's recent murders were committed during struggles over leather coats. Incredibly, a 3-year-old boy took a loaded handgun to a nursery school in Brooklyn this week, becoming perhaps the youngest juvenile to bear firearms in the city's history. In Washington so far this year, more than 60 juveniles have been charged with homicide, a figure similar to that of last year. Yet in the eight previous years, there were only a total of 60 juvenile homicide arrests.

Nationally, homicide arrests of people between the ages of 10 and 17 have climbed sharply since 1984.

The slaughter may be indirectly related to drugs; crack dealing gave countless teen-agers the wherewithal to buy sophisticated guns that now are common features of the adolescent demimonde.

Whatever the cause, the proliferation of powerful weapons demands a strong response. New York's Police Commissioner, Lee Brown, has taken some promising steps, including creating a task force to target groups that import guns from states with lax laws, and cracking down on local abuse of Federal licenses for gun dealers.

There is also a glaring need for more support from Congress, which is now so intimidated by the gun lobby that it resists even popular, sensible laws to limit interstate gun traffic and youngsters' access to firearms.

The need to keep guns from juveniles is at least as obvious as the need to limit their access to drugs and alcohol. As urban bloodshed mounts, perhaps even the gun lobby will acknowledge that children with guns kill people.

Law Professor Accuses Thomas Of Sexual Harassment in 1980s

BY NEIL A. LEWIS | OCT. 7, 1991

In front of an all-male Senate Judiciary Committee, Anita Hill testified to the sexual harassment she allegedly endured from Clarence Thomas, Supreme Court nominee and her former supervisor at the Equal Employment Opportunity Commission. No criminal charges were issued, and Judge Thomas was confirmed to the Supreme Court. However, Ms. Hill's testimony started a national conversation about sexual harassment that helped to determine its legal definition and led to policies and legislation to prevent it.

TWO DAYS BEFORE the Senate is scheduled to vote on his nomination to the Supreme Court, Judge Clarence Thomas was publicly accused today of sexually harassing a law professor at the University of Oklahoma Law Center during the two years she served as his personal assistant in the Federal Government.

Anita F. Hill, a tenured professor of law at Oklahoma, maintained in an affidavit submitted to the Senate Judiciary Committee last month that when she worked for Judge Thomas over a two-year period beginning in 1981, he frequently asked her out and when she refused he spoke to her in detail about pornographic films he had seen.

The allegation added an element of uncertainty to what had already been a turbulent confirmation process for Judge Thomas, who is President Bush's choice to succeed Justice Thurgood Marshall on the Supreme Court.

Senator John C. Danforth, a Missouri Republican who is the 43-year-old nominee's principal supporter in the Senate, said today that Judge Thomas "forcefully denies" the allegations.

Senator Paul Simon, an Illinois Democrat who is a member of the Judiciary Committee, said today that because of the allegations the vote should be delayed. But Senate aides said they expected the vote to go forward because a delay would require the consent of all 100

Anita F. Hill, a tenured professor of law at the University of Oklahoma, accuses Supreme Court nominee Clarence Thomas of sexual harassment during a two-year period when she worked for him.

members. At least 54 Senators have declared their intention to vote to confirm Judge Thomas.

Nonetheless, as word of the allegations spread this weekend, the White House and Judge Thomas's supporters mounted a swift counterattack on several fronts, depicting him as the victim of a desperate final gambit by his opponents.

Professor Hill never filed a formal complaint against Judge Thomas. The accusations were first reported today by Newsday and National Public Radio. NPR said Professor Hill had first made them to the Judiciary Committee the week of Sept. 10, while members of the panel were questioning Judge Thomas in public hearings.

In an interview broadcast this morning on NPR, Professor Hill said she had initially decided that she would not tell the committee of her accusations but changed her mind as the hearings were about to begin because she felt she had an obligation to tell what she believed to be true. "Here is a person who is in charge of protecting rights of women and other groups in the workplace and he is using his position of power for personal gain for one thing," she said. "And he did it in a very ugly and intimidating way."

Senator Joseph R. Biden Jr., the Delaware Democrat who heads the Judiciary Committee, said in a statement today that when Ms. Hill first contacted the committee, on Sept. 12, she insisted that her name not be used and that Judge Thomas not be told of her allegations. He said this effectively tied the committee's hands.

Only on Sept. 23, Mr. Biden said, did she agree to allow the Federal Bureau of Investigation to investigate the allegations. The report was finished by Sept. 25, he said, and all committee members were notified of it by the next day. On Sept. 27, the committee deadlocked 7 to 7 on the nomination.

The White House today described the F.B.I. report as finding the allegations as "without foundation." But Congressional officials who have seen the report said the bureau could not draw any conclusion because of the "he said, she said" nature of the subject.

In her interview with NPR, Professor Hill said that at the time she was being harassed she confided in a law school classmate, a woman who is now a state judge in the West. NPR said the woman confirmed Ms. Hill's account of the content and timing of their conversation on the condition that she not be identified.

By all accounts, the White House and the Senate Democratic leadership, including Senator Biden and Senator George J. Mitchell, the majority leader, were briefed about the accusation shortly after the F.B.I. completed its investigation, which included an interview with the state judge.

In 1981, the time cited by Professor Hill, Judge Thomas headed the Office of Civil Rights in the Department of Education and she was his personal assistant.

In her affidavit, Congressional officials said, Professor Hill said that typically after a brief discussion of work, Judge Thomas would turn the conversations to discussions about his sexual interests. She described his remarks as vivid as he discussed sexual acts he had seen in pornographic films.

Professor Hill, the officials continued, said Judge Thomas, who was separated from his first wife at the time, dropped the sexual talk when he began dating someone else. Since the remarks had stopped, she said, she accepted an offer to follow him as a personal assistant when he became chairman of the Equal Employment Opportunity Commission. There, she said, he soon resumed his advances.

Professor Hill did not return repeated telephone calls seeking comment today. In a written statement sent by fax to news organizations, she said she was first approached by the Judiciary Committee on Sept. 3 and was invited to provide background information on the judge because she had worked with him. She said that after "numerous discussions" with the panel's staff she decided to submit an affidavit.

She said she discussed the matter publicly with the NPR reporter, Nina Totenberg, only because the reporter had a copy of the affidavit and she wanted to be able to respond to the information before it was made public.

FEELING SHE HAD NO CHOICE

In the NPR interview, Professor Hill said Judge Thomas never tried to touch her nor did he directly threaten her job. But she said that at the age of 25 she felt vulnerable and intimidated.

"I felt as though I did not have a choice, that the pressure was such that I was going to have to submit to that pressure in order to continue getting good assignments," she told NPR.

Congressional officials said today that Judge Thomas told F.B.I. investigators that he had asked Ms. Hill out a few times and after she declined eventually dropped all advances.

The lateness of Professor Hill's allegations raised several issues, including the Judiciary Committee's timing and procedures in handling of her accusations. It also illustrated the intensely political nature of modern confirmation battles for the Supreme Court.

ATTACKING HILL'S CREDIBILITY

Senator Danforth said the charges were a desperate "eleventh-hour attack more typical of a political campaign than of a Supreme Court confirmation." In an effort to diminish Professor Hill's credibility, he said that Judge Thomas flew out to Norman, Okla., this spring to address her law students at her invitation.

Senator Orrin G. Hatch, Republican Utah, suggested that one of his colleagues, whom he did not name, violated Senate rules by leaking the report to the news media, The Associated Press reported.

A White House official said Ms. Hill's credibility was damaged by the fact that she did not make these allegations until very late in the confirmation process, nine years after the alleged acts occurred.

The White House provided reporters with the name of Phyllis Berry, who worked with both Ms. Hill and Mr. Thomas at the employment opportunity commission as its Congressional liaison officer. In an interview, Ms. Berry suggested that the allegations were a result of Ms. Hill's disappointment and frustration that Mr. Thomas did not show any sexual interest in her. Ms. Berry speculated that because Judge Thomas was "not able to respond to her in the way she expected or hoped, he might have hurt her feelings."

SUPPORT FROM COLLEAGUES

But a number of colleagues and friends of Ms. Hill said they could not imagine her fabricating such allegations. "I've known Anita Hill for 14 years and she is a person of enormous integrity and spirituality," said Stephen L. Carter, a law professor at Yale University who attended Yale Law School with Professor Hill.

Prof. Harry F. Tepker Jr., a colleague of Professor Hill at the University of Oklahoma, issued a statement saying: "Anita is not part of any political plot. I share the view of those who say that Judge Thomas has been subjected to unfair criticism in the past, but that is not the case here. In my view, Anita's disclosures have nothing to do with partisanship or politics."

In the NPR interview, Professor Hill said that in 1983, Judge Thomas told her that if she ever "made a statement about his behavior" it would be "enough to ruin his career." She said, "My response was that I really just wanted to leave the experience behind me."

At the time Ms. Hill asserts the harassment took place, Judge Thomas, as chairman of the E.E.O.C., was in effect the nation's chief enforcement officer on sexual harassment claims.

The courts have only recently viewed sexual harassment as a legal issue, and now recognize two types. The first is found when a supervisor or employer makes sexual advances and links it to promotion or continued employment. The second, more subtle form, involves actions by a supervisor that create an unwelcome or hostile work environment.

In 1986, the Supreme Court ruled in a unanimous decision that severe or pervasive sexual harassment of an employee by a supervisor constituted a violation of Federal law. Even before that ruling set a nationwide standard, it had been the law in the District of Columbia since 1977.

In interviews with NPR and Newsday for the initial news reports, Senator Simon complained that he had not been informed of the allegations of sexual harassment before the committee's vote.

But today, Mr. Simon appeared to contradict his earlier account by acknowledging that he was aware of the allegations and had even spoken to Ms. Hill before the vote. Asked to explain the difference, Senator Simon said he simply forgot that he had been informed of Ms. Hill's allegations.

Senator Simon said that he had spoken with Ms. Hill shortly before the committee voted and that he had found her a credible witness. "I did not have the feeling that this was somebody doing this as a lark to get publicity or that sort of thing," he said.

Why Some Get Busted —
and Some Go Free

OPINION | BY BRENT STAPLES | MAY 10, 1999

DRUG ARRESTS on the 10 o'clock news tend to show inner-city blacks and Latinos being led away in handcuffs. But Federal health statistics show only slight differences in the rates of drug use for whites and people of color — and define the typical drug addict as a white male in his 20's who lives in a suburb where drug busts almost never happen.

The Partnership for a Drug-Free America expects to spend nearly $200 million this year to convince policy makers and affluent Americans that the drug problem crosses racial, economic and geographic lines. This point would seem self-evident. But the myth that drug use is confined to the black inner city will be difficult to dislodge.

The Hartford Courant learned how deep the myth runs when it published a series in 1992 that examined the lives of drug addicts who supported their habits through prostitution. Conditioned to think of drug abuse as a minority problem, some readers were stunned that 70 percent of the drug-addicted prostitutes shown in the series turned out to be white. Some doubted that the story was true. The refusal to believe that white heroin addicts exist was particularly self-deceptive in a state that is almost 90 percent white.

The same stereotypes have been at play for decades along the mid-Atlantic stretch of Interstate 95, where the presumed link between race and drugs has led state troopers to stop and search black motorists based on race alone. The profiling scandal in New Jersey is spreading. Last week Boston opened a profiling investigation of its own.

The move in Boston was helped along by a Federal judge who sharply cut the expected sentence for a black man who had been charged with weapons possession after a random traffic stop. Judge Nancy Gertner chastised the police, saying that nothing in the man's record or driving conduct justified them in stopping him.

Turning to the police record, the judge found a host of random stops. She noted that "African-American motorists are stopped and prosecuted for traffic stops more than any other citizens" and suggested they were "imprisoned at a higher rate for these offenses as well." Citing "deep concerns" about the disparity, the judge gave the man 30 months, when she could have given him six years.

Statistics from Maryland and New Jersey show that black motorists are about five times as likely to be stopped on the highway as whites. Even Americans who disapprove of racial profiling tend to view it as a passing humiliation, with no broad social import. But criminologists have long argued that profiling goes well beyond the personal and exerts a substantial impact on the criminal justice process and the broader social order as well.

Speaking at a national conference last week, Dr. Dawn Day, an addiction specialist from the Dogwood Center in Princeton, N.J., drew a connection between racial profiling of intravenous drug users and the rapid spread of AIDS in the black community.

The most conservative estimates suggest that white intravenous drug users outnumber black users by at least 5 to 1. Even so, drug sweeps tend to be concentrated in inner cities, which are widely viewed as the sole source of the problem. Dr. Day's calculations, based on Federal data, show 5 arrests for every 100 white addicts, but 20 arrests for every 100 black addicts.

Unworried about random searches and arrests, many white addicts carry clean needles so that they can avoid sharing needles and the risk of getting AIDS. But black addicts know that they are vulnerable to random search and arrest and often choose not to carry needles. Instead, they share the needles of strangers, getting AIDS and other blood-borne diseases in the process. As a consequence, the rate of H.I.V. infection for black drug users is many times that of whites.

Criminologists have argued for decades that racial profiling plays a central role in the fact that black Americans make up a disproportionate part of the prison population. Drug cartels have long since grasped this point, minimizing the use of non-whites as couriers and using people who look like mild-mannered suburban housewives whenever possible.

Police departments have historically justified profiling by arguing that it leads to valid arrests. But the practice also exempts from scrutiny the vast majority of drug users and couriers who are by definition non-black. The race-based practice catches some of the guilty, but it violates the lives of many more innocent people, undermining law-enforcement credibility in minority neighborhoods. Finally, the myth that drug crime is a "black" problem, confined to ghettos, allows the culture to deceive itself about the vast scope of the epidemic.

Daughter's Death Prompts Fight on 'Date Rape' Drug

BY KEITH BRADSHER | OCT. 16, 1999

ROCKWOOD, MICH., OCT. 16 — Students from the Oscar Carlson High School here say that when they go to parties these days, they try to keep an eye on their drinks at all times, put caps back on bottled beverages between sips and never accept a cup from someone they do not know.

The precautions follow the death last January of Samantha Reid, a 15-year-old freshman who drank a glass of Mountain Dew laced with GHB, an increasingly popular recreational and "date rape" drug that is colorless, odorless and virtually tasteless. Samantha's death, one of 49 linked to the drug nationwide since 1990, has galvanized an effort to crack down on GHB, gamma hydroxybutyrate.

Two Michigan Republicans, Representative Fred Upton and Senator Spencer Abraham, have sponsored bills in the House and Senate that would add GHB to the Federal Government's list of the most-controlled substances, joining heroin and LSD as a so-called Schedule 1 drug. The House passed its bill on Tuesday by a vote of 423 to 1 with little debate. The Senate bill, introduced two months ago, is in committee but is also expected to win passage. The bills would make GHB trafficking punishable by a sentence of five years to life in prison.

The bills would ban not only GHB but also similar chemical compounds, including some dietary supplements for body builders that can be used to make the drug. GHB "is easily synthesized by a lot of people who can get the recipe off the Internet," said Dr. Felix Adatsi, the chief toxicologist of the Michigan State Police. "It can be made in a kitchen."

Small quantities of the drug produce a temporary euphoria or sometimes hallucinations, while slightly larger quantities produce lassitude, unconsciousness or even respiratory failure and death. The drug can be lethal in even tiny doses, or if poorly prepared. Doctors recommend that a person rendered unconscious by GHB receive immediate care by an ambulance crew or emergency room doctors who have been told to suspect the drug's presence.

Samantha was an average student who loved to play basketball at Carlson High in this small factory town on the southern outskirts of Detroit. She encountered the drug on a Saturday night when her mother thought she was at a movie. Instead, Samantha and two other freshman girls joined four young men, two of whom were seniors at Carlson, and went to the apartment of one of the men to watch rented videos.

Her mother, Judi Clark, was summoned in the middle of the night to the local hospital, where she found her daughter dead.

"I fell asleep on the couch and was woken up by the phone at 3 or 3:30," said Ms. Clark, who resumed using her maiden name after her divorce from Samantha's father in 1986. Ms. Clark reared Samantha and Samantha's older brother, Charles, now 18.

Douglas M. Baker, the Wayne County deputy chief prosecutor for drug crimes, said that one of the young men at the party with Samantha, Joshua Cole, 19, later told the police that he had secretly put GHB into all three girls' drinks to make the party more "lively." Mr. Cole also told the police that two of the other three young men had agreed to the plan and helped carry the drinks to the girls, Mr. Baker said.

Samantha died a few hours later. One of her friends went into a coma but was revived. The third girl never touched her drink. All four men, ranging in age now from 18 to 26, have been charged with involuntary manslaughter and poisoning, and, if convicted, could be sentenced to life in prison. Mr. Cole and the other three young men have pleaded not guilty. Lawyers for the other three young men have contended that Mr. Cole was solely responsible for the death. Mr. Cole has denied this.

Ms. Clark has turned her daughter's death into a crusade for limits on GHB. She took six months off from her job as a unionized construction worker after Samantha's death to study the drug and write letters to politicians seeking controls on it.

Ms. Clark has not touched her daughter's room. Samantha had strewn clothes on her bed and floor in choosing what to wear when she went out on the night she died. The clothes are still there. So are the black lava lamp, the white strobe lamp, the posters of Leonardo DiCaprio and the movie "Titanic," the herd of stuffed animals and the piles of teen-age magazines.

"I haven't even dusted," Ms. Clark said. "It's just like the night she left, except more dust."

Michigan is not alone in having a GHB problem. The use of the drug has been spreading in New York, California, Florida, Pennsylvania and other states. According to the Drug Enforcement Administration, hospitals and law-enforcement officials have reported at least 5,500 cases of GHB abuse in 42 states, in addition to the 49 deaths, 5 of which occurred in Michigan.

Yet no one is certain of the true extent of the problem. Because GHB is not yet on the Federal list of controlled substances, the Drug Enforcement Administration does not actively pursue cases involving it, said E. David Jacobson, an agency spokesman. The agency has helped with local investigations in some of the 29 states where the drug is a controlled substance, including Michigan.

GHB breaks down quickly in the body and is extremely difficult for laboratories to detect even before it breaks down. Only four laboratories in the country even have the equipment to detect GHB, and they can do so only if a blood or urine sample is gathered within a few hours after the drug is ingested, Dr. Adatsi said.

Because kits for making GHB are illegal in Michigan but legal in many other states, the state attorney general's office reached across state lines to combat it. The office bought kits over the Internet from two vendors in Florida and Colorado last summer, then filed criminal charges against the two men and extradited them for trial here. They have pleaded not guilty.

GHB prosecutions are "an extremely high priority, in that this substance has popped up at these rave parties, and kids can't detect it in a drink," said Jennifer M. Granholm, Michigan's Attorney General. Ms. Granholm added that she planned to speak on the subject when the nation's state attorneys general gather in January for a conference on Internet-related crimes.

Gamma hydroxybutyrate is a highly addictive chemical compound that depresses the central nervous system. Toxicologists say that in precise quantities, with the ingredients prepared in carefully measured ratios, GHB produces a mild euphoria followed by sleep, with no hangover.

But GHB is seldom prepared with clinical care or administered in precise amounts. Kitchen chemists use extremely caustic liquids like paint remover, furniture polish remover or drain clearing agents to prepare the drug, which, when poorly mixed, can cause severe chemical burns to a user's throat. The drug is also such a powerful sedative that an error in dosage of a tiny fraction of a gram can cause a coma and eventually death.

Because GHB can render someone unconscious or unable to remember what happens next, the drug has been used for several years by sexual predators across the country, who put it in women's drinks, Mr. Jacobson said. But more recently, young people have been taking the drug more often for the euphoria it can produce, and in the mistaken belief among men that it builds muscles, toxicologists say.

There is no evidence of sexual misconduct in the Samantha Reid case, Mr. Baker said. Her death now appears to have been an early warning for the state, because overdoses have become more frequent since. Eight people overdosed on GHB in one weekend three weeks ago in Ann Arbor. While some overdoses since Samantha's have produced temporary comas, none nave been fatal.

While Ms. Clark has returned to work, installing heating ducts in new office buildings and factories, she continues her fight against GHB in the evenings.

"I'm trying as hard as I can to make some purpose out of my daughter's death," Ms. Clark said. "She can't die without a purpose, or I'd go out of my mind."

CHAPTER 5

The 2000s and Beyond

Despite the recent spate of mass shootings, violent crimes such as homicide and assault are today at historic lows across the United States. However, crimes such as fraud, insider trading and money laundering have increased in frequency. Hacking is a growing threat. And sexual harassment is now acknowledged as criminal behavior, though the precise definition of harassment and its appropriate punishment are still widely debated.

U.S. Officials Lay Out Plan To Fight Computer Attacks

BY DAVID JOHNSTON | **FEB. 17, 2000**

A WEEK AFTER unidentified hackers paralyzed several commercial Internet companies, the country's chief law enforcement and legal officers said today that threats against computer networks had outstripped the government's efforts to keep up with them.

Testifying before a Senate panel on Internet security, the attorney general, Janet Reno, said that last week's attacks on popular World Wide Web sites illustrated the necessity of a coordinated law enforcement strategy. "How we deal with cybercrime is one of the most critical areas we face," Ms. Reno said.

Ms. Reno proposed a five-year plan that would include tougher penalties for hackers and standardized investigative technologies. Such a step could lower the astronomical cost of security and detection gear in an environment in which, she said, equipment is obsolete almost as soon as it is installed.

Louis J. Freeh, the F.B.I. director, told senators that the investigation of last week's attacks was moving aggressively.

"There are fast-developing leads as we speak," Mr. Freeh said of the search for those who barraged the computer systems of companies like Yahoo, eBay and Amazon.com with meaningless data to clog the paths of customers trying to reach the sites.

He said that the investigation was being conducted in the United States as well as in Germany and Canada. Scores of agents from F.B.I. offices in Atlanta, Boston, Los Angeles, San Francisco and Seattle are at work on the attacks, known within law enforcement circles as "distributed denial of service" cases.

Separately, law enforcement officials have said they are interviewing several people, including some computer hackers, although they did not yet have evidence clearly indicating who was responsible for the disruptive attacks.

Underscoring the seriousness of the problem, Mr. Freeh cited the growing number of such cases, to 1,154 last year from 547 in 1998. The cases range from minor attacks by teenage vandals and disgruntled employees to highly sophisticated intrusions possibly directed by foreign intelligence services, he said.

Mr. Freeh said that in 1998, 399 cases were closed, in contrast to 1999, when 912 cases closed. Almost no case resulted in prosecutions. The F.B.I. closes a case when the agency decides there is no basis for further investigation. The cases do not include other major categories of cybercrime, like Internet fraud or child pornography.

The testimony by Ms. Reno and Mr. Freeh followed a White House meeting convened on Tuesday by President Clinton with technology experts and Internet executives about how to improve the security of the country's computer networks. Mr. Clinton adopted a reassuring tone.

Some industry officials have said they want strong action against computer criminals but fear that Government intervention and new criminal laws could unintentionally stifle the phenomenal growth and creativity of the technology industries.

Expanding on the President's request for an extra $37 million for the Justice Department to enforce computer security, Ms. Reno said that the money would include $4 million for 59 new assistant United States attorneys and 9 additional attorneys in the criminal division to prosecute computer and child pornography crimes; $8.7 million for training for state and local law enforcement agencies; and $11.4 million for 100 new F.B.I. computer analysis and response team members.

In addition, she told the committee, "we intend to enhance law enforcement's ability to deal with evidence available on computers by developing up to 10 new regional computer forensic labs."

Aftermath of Internet Pedophilia Case: Guilt, and a New Awareness of Danger

BY DEBRA WEST | JULY 12, 2000

FIRST THERE WERE cryptic notes left next to the computer. Then phone calls in the middle of the night. Sometimes, half asleep, she would hear the front door gently closing and someone whispering in the driveway. By the time she got up, her son would be gone. Off again with the high school's bad crowd, she supposed at first. Out of control.

Later, she realized he was a victim of Internet pedophiles. But it was only after another boy, a 12-year-old named Orlandito Rosario Maldonado, was found buried along the Saw Mill River Parkway, and the police told her about it, that the woman discovered in how much danger her 15-year-old son had really been.

"I don't know if he was incredibly naive, or bent on self-destruction or sexually addicted to the Internet, or what," the mother said of her son, who was sexually abused by several middle-aged men he met through an Internet chat room. One of the men was Robert D. DeRosario, a convicted child abuser whom the police have identified as the main suspect in Orlandito's killing.

The two boys lived a few miles and several worlds apart. One was wealthy and skilled in computers, pointing and clicking his way to disaster. The other, Orlandito, was simply unlucky. They never met, but the boys were linked to each other and to an unlikely group of successful suburban men by a criminal investigation that is a reminder of how technology can bring different people and diverse worlds together for worse, as well as for better.

For the past year, a wide-ranging investigation into Internet pedophilia has cast Westchester County in a surreal new light that is part David Lynch, part Wired magazine. In all, nine middle-aged men have been convicted of or pleaded guilty to sexually abusing boys as young as 13 whom they met through the Internet. The defendants include a Yonkers city official, a former member of the Somers school board, a former chairman of the New Castle planning board and a retired spokesman for PepsiCo Inc.

The police had not set out to arrest pedophiles. That happened almost by accident. Their investigation was intended to solve the killing of Orlandito.

"We opened up Pandora's box," said Lt. Christopher Calabrese, commander of the Major Case Squad of the Westchester County Police. "You like to think you have your finger on the pulse of the county, and then you come across this. It gives you a different perspective."

Orlandito, a sixth grader from Yonkers, disappeared on Nov. 2, 1998, after he skipped on a haircut appointment and went to buy a toy laser pointer.

His body was discovered nearly three months later, on Jan. 23, 1999, next to an abandoned ice cream stand along the parkway in Dobbs Ferry.

A skinny boy with curly black hair, Orlandito loved football and loved having a few extra dollars in his pocket. Too young to work legally, he hung around a local supermarket and delivered groceries for tips.

But his experience with the digital age began and ended with Nintendo. He had never even been on the Internet, so it is odd that his death would set off a high-tech cybercrime investigation.

From the beginning, however, Mr. DeRosario, 37, a carpenter who lived just two blocks from Orlandito, was considered a suspect in the killing, the police said. Orlandito was last seen alive in Mr. DeRosario's apartment building, the police say. Mr. DeRosario has not been charged with the killing, but the investigation is focused on him.

As part of the investigation, the police seized Mr. DeRosario's computer and quickly discovered a gay men's chat room that they said he frequented under the screen name BobbyD63.

That America Online chat room, WestchesterNYm4m, is reminiscent of pre-AIDS bathhouses: it is anonymous, it is local and it is largely about arranging in-person sexual encounters. The men who enter the chat room display personal profiles that sum up their characteristics and desires in a direct way. Few of the participants appeared interested in pedophilia. On a recent night, a "6-foot-2 slim Italian" signed on, saying he was interested in meeting "fat or chubby black men," while a man who called himself "Tarrytown" was less discriminating: he wanted to meet anyone who was "up for hot fun tomorrow eve."

It was in this chat room that a troubled teenager, who was struggling in school, socially unpopular and questioning his own sexuality, found the men who would rush at the chance to abuse him, his mother said. For nearly a year, from the spring of 1998, when he was 14, to January 1999, when his parents sent him away to boarding school, this boy, who had once loved tennis and been commended by his teachers for his talent as a peer counselor, became a chat room regular.

His profile said that he liked older men, and the feeding frenzy began.

"I think these people got him when he was vulnerable," said his mother, who agreed to be interviewed on the condition that her name and where she lives not be revealed. "He didn't have a lot of interests. He wasn't involved in high school life at all. He was getting bad grades. He was coming home in the afternoon and spending all of his time on the computer."

All nine of the men who were prosecuted in the sex-crimes investigation after Orlandito's killing preyed on the 15-year-old boy, though some were also charged with abusing other boys. The boy gave statements to the police implicating all nine and testified in the one case that went to trial. Two other boys gave statements implicating separate men. Police investigators insist there were many other victims whom they could not persuade to come forward and provide evidence for the prosecution.

Mr. DeRosario pleaded guilty in May to abusing 12 boys, including the 15-year-old. Under his plea agreement, he will get 10 years in prison when he is sentenced in July. His lawyer, Vincent Lanna, did not return several phone calls seeking comment about the plea or about Orlandito's death.

"DeRosario basically had two pools of boys: one, boys from the neighborhood who would appreciate a dollar or a present, and the other, boys he met on the Internet," Lieutenant Calabrese said. The investigation into Orlandito's killing continues, but the police believe that the boy fit into the first of those pools.

They were two pools that could not have been further apart.

By the time Chief George N. Longworth of the Dobbs Ferry police visited the family of the 15-year-old to ask what their son might know about Orlandito's murder, the boy's parents had already sent him away to school.

They knew their son was involved with middle-aged men he had met on the Internet, but the youth officer of their community's police department had advised against reporting the abuse to the sex crimes bureau, mistakenly saying that if they did, their names would be in the police blotter, available for anyone to see. They decided to get the boy help privately rather than try to prosecute the men who abused him.

When Chief Longworth showed up with questions about a killing, the boy's parents realized their son faced more danger than they had ever imagined.

They persuaded him to cooperate with the police, though at first the boy was very reluctant to do so, the mother said.

"He thought he was in love with these men," the mother said with regret. She noted that her son took a laptop computer on family vacations and could unobtrusively send e-mail messages to them from wherever he was. "Obviously the state of your mind when you're a teenager can be swayed so."

Many of the men her son was involved with were prominent locally. They had professional credentials and admirable civic commitment, and some have long-running marriages. Some of the men who were arrested had chatted regularly with others online using their screen names, and the boy they abused gossiped about some of them with others, but the men did not appear to know one another, the police said.

Two of them tried to reach the boy even as their cases were in court, his mother said.

Mr. DeRosario called the family's home from jail just before the boy was scheduled to testify in the trial of Walter Salvatore, 39, a Staten Island man, who was convicted of sending the boy pictures of himself naked and faces sodomy charges after taking the boy to a Staten Island motel.

Patrick Murphy, 45, the Pepsico executive, has sent letters to the family home since the boy has been away. Mr. Murphy, who is H.I.V.-positive and admitted having unprotected sex with the boy, has pleaded guilty to reckless endangerment as well as to sodomy charges. The boy's mother said her son was H.I.V.-negative. The letters, she said, she turned over to the police.

If she could give a warning to other parents about the dangers of the Internet, the woman said it would be this: keep computers children use in a shared part of the house; limit computer time; and, most important, make sure children are involved in activities after school.

In the menacing southwest corner of Yonkers where Orlandito lived with his father, Jose Rosario, and three brothers in a fourth floor walk-up, the feeling is that Internet access ought to be denied to children, not just regulated. Orlandito's parents are separated. His father, who moved to Yonkers from Puerto Rico five years before the murder and does not speak English, has moved since Orlandito's death and was not reachable for comment.

But others in this hilly Nodine Hill neighborhood said they still felt the loss. Sharon Simon, who lived downstairs from Orlandito and often comforted him when he complained of missing his mother, who is in Puerto Rico, said he was a considerate child who was well liked by the neighbors.

"It's a shame," Ms. Simon said. "He was a good boy." From his death and the news stories linking him to the Internet pedophile investigation, young mothers in the neighborhood, who sigh and shake their heads over how cute Orlandito was, have concluded that the Internet is no place for children.

"I'm not having my kids on the Internet," said Di'Maina Ballinger, 28, a mother of three who lives in Nodine Hill. "They just got three new computers in school — blue, pink, green — they're beautiful. They sent a form home from school asking, 'Can your child use the Internet.' I just said no."

But despite her advice to other parents in an interview, the 15-year-old boy's mother is so protective of the family's privacy that she has told few friends about her son's troubles, and even her own daughter has not been told the truth about what happened or why her brother was sent to a boarding school.

"It's hard, I have all these alibis," she said. "My husband is an extremely private person. I think he feels even more like a failure than I do as a parent. And I feel like a failure as a parent."

Try as they might, however, the pedophilia scandal is a difficult subject to avoid.

Commuters sometimes joke about the cases, on the Metro-North train, not realizing that a primary victim's father is among them. The mother has excused herself from dinner parties when neighbors smirk and say that they always suspected that one of the more prominent men who pleaded guilty in the case was gay.

"It's my son they are talking about," she said.

Prominent Trader Accused of Defrauding Clients

BY THE NEW YORK TIMES | DEC. 11, 2008

BERNARD L. MADOFF, a legend among Wall Street traders, was arrested on Thursday by federal agents and charged with criminal securities fraud stemming from his company's money management business, The New York Times's Diana B. Henriques and Zachery Kouwe report.

The arrest and criminal complaint were confirmed just before 6 p.m. Thursday by Lev L. Dassin, the acting United States attorney in Manhattan, and Mark Mershon, the assistant director of the Federal Bureau of Investigation.

According to the complaint, Mr. Madoff advised colleagues at the firm on Wednesday that his investment advisory business was "all just one big lie" that was "basically, a giant Ponzi scheme" that, by his estimate, had lost $50 billion over many years.

Related accusations were made in a lawsuit filed by the Securities and Exchange Commission in federal court in Manhattan. That complaint accuses Mr. Madoff of defrauding advisory clients of his firm and seeks emergency relief to protect potential victims, including an asset freeze and the appointment of a receiver for the firm.

"We are alleging a massive fraud — both in terms of scope and duration," said Linda Chatman Thomsen, director of the S.E.C. enforcement division. "We are moving quickly and decisively to stop the fraud and protect remaining assets for investors."

Another regulator, Andrew M. Calamari, the associate director of enforcement in the New York Regional S.E.C. Office, said the case involved "a stunning fraud that appears to be of epic proportions."

Although not a household name among consumers, Mr. Madoff's firm has played a significant role in the structure of Wall Street for decades, both in traditional stock trading and in the development of newer electronic networks for trading equities and derivatives.

The S.E.C.'s complaint, filed in federal court in Manhattan, alleges that Mr. Madoff informed two senior employees on Wednesday that his investment advisory business was a fraud. Mr. Madoff told these employees that he was "finished," that he had "absolutely nothing."

The senior employees understood him to be saying that he had for years been paying returns to certain investors out of the principal received from other, different investors. Mr. Madoff admitted in this conversation that the firm was insolvent and had been for years, and that he estimated the losses from this fraud were at least $50 billion, according to the regulatory complaint.

Mr. Madoff, 70, founded Bernard L. Madoff Investment Securities in 1960 and liked to recount how he had earned his initial stake by working as a life guard at city beaches and installing underground sprinkler systems. By the early 1980s, his firm was one of the largest independent trading operations in the securities industry.

The company had around $300 million in assets in 2000 at the height of the Internet bubble and ranked among the top trading and securities firms in the nation. Mr. Madoff ran the business with several family-members including his brother Peter, his nephew Charles, his niece, Shana and his sons Mark and Andrew.

Reached at his office, Peter Madoff declined to comment.

The alleged scheme apparently involved an asset-management unit of Madoff Securities, which Mr. Madoff started after the market-making business became difficult once stocks started being quoted in decimals instead of fractions

Mr. Madoff is currently on the board of Nasdaq OMX Group, formerly the Nasdaq Stock Market, and serves as the chairman of the Sy Syms School of Business at Yeshiva University. His son Mark Madoff served as the vice chairman of the board of directors of the National Association of Securities Dealers, from 1993 to 1994 and was also an board member of brokerage firm A.G. Edwards.

His firm, which at one point was the largest market maker on the electronic Nasdaq Stock Market, employed hundreds of traders.

Ponzi Scheme Meets Ransomware for a Doubly Malicious Attack

BY SHEERA FRENKEL | JUNE 6, 2017

SAN FRANCISCO — The first message to pop up on the computer screen let the victims know they had been hacked. The second message gave them a way out.

The victim had a choice: Pay the hackers a ransom of one bitcoin, a digital currency worth roughly $2,365, in exchange for regaining access to the computer, or try to infect two new people on behalf of the attackers. If someone the victim knew fell for the bait and became infected, the attackers would consider the ransom paid and cede control of the infected computer.

The attack late last year was, according to the cybersecurity researchers who discovered what they now call the Popcorn Time ransomware, the first Ponzi scheme for one of the internet's oldest types of cyberattacks.

Ransomware, a type of malicious software that infects a system and then holds it hostage, demanding a ransom for its release, is one of the most popular and lucrative ways to attack computers.

Security companies estimate that criminals raked in roughly $1 billion from ransomware attacks in 2016. This year, the number is likely to be much higher, as ransomware schemes multiply. One strain, WannaCry, made global headlines last month by infecting hundreds of thousands of computers in 74 countries in about a day.

The scheme has become more successful as more of what we do goes online, from business client lists to family photos. With the click of a button, an entire system can be infected. With another click, criminals can wipe information from a computer or expose it to the public. It all depends on what commands a bigger ransom: losing information or exposing it.

Security researchers warn that WannaCry, which exploited a wide ranging vulnerability in Windows systems and then used a clever

mechanism to spread itself across new systems, is just the tip of the iceberg. They are tracking new schemes dreamed up by criminals who have quickly realized that people are willing to pay hundreds, if not thousands, of dollars in ransom.

"This is a growing business because it works," said Mikko Hypponen, chief research officer at F-Secure, a security firm based in Helsinki, Finland. "And the attacks are becoming more creative and effective."

Mr. Hypponen, whose team found and first reported on the Popcorn malware, said it was an outlier in the world of ransomware. It was the first attempt to combine a Ponzi, or pyramid scheme, in which one person entraps another, with malware that holds a computer hostage for payment. If it proved successful, he added, a number of criminal networks were likely to copy the model. Researchers are still monitoring the scheme to see if it works.

"These networks all watch each other and learn. When a new model works, it quickly grows as others build on it," Mr. Hypponen said.

Asaf Cidon, a vice president at the security company Barracuda Networks who studies ransomware, said that criminals had become more sophisticated in the last year, especially in how they choose their victims.

"Attackers will go after a specific department at a company, for instance human resources, where they know emails and links are more likely to get opened," Mr. Cidon said. Networks will choose a company to target and then comb LinkedIn to draw a map of people employed by that company, he said.

They might then use that map to impersonate various people or leverage their way into the company's social network, ultimately using whatever means necessary to make sure that the system becomes infected with the ransomware.

"We've seen them impersonate people within the company, or impersonate airlines sending ticketing information or vendors and customers of the company sending files," Mr. Cidon said, adding that all businesses, from mom-and-pop shops to giant Silicon Valley companies like Facebook and Google, were getting hit by ransomware attacks.

Other notable ransomware schemes discovered recently included a plot to infect internet-connected home devices, such as the LG Smart TV, by displaying a fake F.B.I. warning screen on the television and demanding $500 to unlock the it.

Late last year, researchers carried out a proof-of-concept demonstration showing how internet-connected home thermostats, such as Nest, could be hacked and held hostage, leaving homeowners in the freezing cold (or blistering heat).

"There is a lot of money at stake here, so criminals are always going to be interested," said Mr. Hypponen, whose company is still tracking the fallout from last month's WannaCry virus.

Though the speed and effectiveness through which that particular attack spread caused it to make headlines, Mr. Hypponen said it was, in ransomware terms, unsuccessful.

"WannaCry was a failure because it became too public, too visible and it made almost no money," said Hypponen, citing the most recent figures that the ransomware netted just under $100,000 for the attackers, who have not yet been caught. WannaCry, he explained, was a victim of its own success. The more public it became, the more unlikely it was that a potential victim would pay out the ransom.

He also said it was an innovative idea, as the attackers combined ransomware with malware that acted like an old internet scourge known as a "worm," essentially spreading itself across systems as it infected them.

While the first worm was created in 1988 by a Cornell graduate student named Robert Morris, who appeared to be more motivated by curiosity than malice, computer worms quickly became one of the most popular and destructive forms of cyberattacks.

"This was a good idea, to combine the two processes together," Mr. Hypponen said. "Other groups are watching this, and we are going to see other versions of this, better versions, soon."

The White-Collar-Crime Cheat Sheet: How the Biggest Scammers Get Away With It.

BY JAIME LOWE | MAY 3, 2018

THE PHRASE "white-collar crime" was in its infancy when the criminologist Edwin Sutherland made it his own. In the late 1930s theft was almost entirely associated with the poor. As he saw it, his fellow sociologists had come to the conclusion that crime was a result of "feeblemindedness, psychopathic deviations, slum neighborhoods and 'deteriorated' families"; it was believed that less than 2 percent of crime came from members of the upper echelons of society. But Sutherland believed this outlook was not only biased, but blinkered, failing to take into account theft that was taking place in plain sight. "The 'robber barons' of the last half of the 19th century were white-collar criminals," he told the crowd of the American Sociological Society in 1939, recounting the time Commodore Cornelius Vanderbilt more or less confessed that his family wealth was ill gotten, saying, "You don't suppose you can run a railroad in accordance with the statutes, do you?"

According to people on both sides of the law, today, thanks to the internet and tax havens, it is even easier for white-collar crime to slip under the radar: Cash is stashed in untouchable island accounts; corporate checks can be forged and deposited; money laundering takes the form of a prepaid debit card; insider trading is just a conversation over cocktails. You'll be shocked to learn just how simple it is to rob and steal while maintaining a veneer of respectability.

CHECK FRAUD

Checks can be useful tools when it comes to engaging in both corporate theft and what are called account takeovers. Each requires a basic understanding of forgery. To steal from a business, says Frank

Abagnale, whose criminal exploits inspired the movie "Catch Me if You Can," the best forgers "capture a corporate logo and maybe the front of the building — layer it in the background, and you can make a check 10 times better looking than the actual check." Then they call the company and ask to speak to someone in accounts receivable. After they explain that they want to pay an invoice by wiring money to the institution, they are told where it does its banking and are given its routing and account numbers. They add that information to the fake check.

Next they find someone in corporate communications to give them a press statement, which will include the signature of the C.E.O. or C.F.O. They scan the document and print the signature onto the check. It is not likely to be scrutinized unless the amount is more than $2,000. "No human being sees the check — it goes through a high-speed processor," Abagnale says. For the last 40 years, he has been a consultant to financial institutions and government agencies, telling them how to combat forgery. Around 17 billion checks, with a value of roughly $27 trillion, were written in 2015, according to the Federal Reserve.

Another, more common way to use checks fraudulently is to take over an individual's account. "Let's say you gave me a check for $9," Abagnale says. "All I would do is go to checksinthemail.com — they have every style of check you can imagine." It's possible for fraudsters to match the style of check they've been given — to duplicate the trees in the background, say — and then to order with a different name on the check along with the bank account information of the unsuspecting person. When the other person's bank receives those checks, it will debit that account. The swindler can pay rent and credit-card bills or visit a local check-cashing operation and walk away with thousands of dollars. "It's months later that anyone would discover it," Abagnale says. "And the bank is responsible for paying both parties even if the business files a complaint within 30 days."

PUMP AND DUMP

Scammers have long mounted schemes to pressure gullible customers to buy assets, especially penny stocks, with promises of hot tips and inside information. But today, the pump-and-dump playbook is being applied to the new frontier of cryptocurrency. "One of the things we're seeing in the virtual-currency space is an application of these old schemes to new conduct," says James McDonald, the director of enforcement for the U.S. Commodity Futures Trading Commission. What pump-and-dump schemes need is a thinly traded market where a price swing is easy to manipulate and disproportionately large compared with how little the asset costs. "If I buy a hundred shares of Apple, that's not going to move the price," McDonald says. "But if there's a new currency, if I buy a hundred tokens or shares, that could be 50 percent of the trading for that day. If it was trading at 10 cents, that could triple the price or more."

The scammers begin by investing a large sum in a currency that is relatively unknown. Then they spread misinformation on social media, claiming, say, that a famous investor like Warren Buffett is investing in the currency. They might post false news articles that say it has been granted a line of credit by bank or a company like Mastercard, and then circulate links to the fake news on social media — spreading the news on Twitter accounts known to promote stocks, for example. It's a risk if the stories are too appealing. An article claiming that the Fed chairman is endorsing an unknown currency for the Reserve or that the United States is going to use a specific coin will not be believed.

Scammers often cultivate an online identity on Twitter or Facebook that becomes known for specializing in recommending currencies or stock picks — then recommend the one they want to pump up and wait for followers to buy it. "Then you have trading that corroborates the misinformation," McDonald says. "You get the false reports, the currency spikes and then it looks believable." Monitoring the en thusiasm for the currency, they sell when it seems to be at a peak. Because they hold the majority of the currency, its price will plummet once they dump the holdings. "This can happen in a matter of minutes," he says.

OFFSHORE TAX HAVEN

People who want to keep their money away from the tax collector will move it to a foreign country. Those who are rich enough will hardly even have to seek out such a tax haven — the opportunities will come to them. "When you have more than $20 million, then you're going to start being targeted by these financial institutions — you will be invited to sporting events like golf or galas," says Gabriel Zucman, an assistant professor of economics at the University of California, Berkeley, and the author of "The Hidden Wealth of Nations." "They won't sell in an aggressive way, but they will talk about legal tax immunization and strategies."

Until the financial crash in 2008, according to Zucman's research, Switzerland controlled approximately 50 percent of the "offshore" accounts used by the world's wealthiest; today that figure is roughly 25 percent. More wealth is now stored in Asia: Singapore and Hong Kong are home to 30 percent of offshore accounts in use, while the rest are in the Caribbean, Panama and Europe.

A lawyer or financial adviser can set up a shell corporation. "There are intermediaries — law firms that can connect people to banks, and they supply these anonymous shell companies," Zucman says. Once the shell company is established, it will send an invoice for phony services like investment advice. Payment for these services then goes to the offshore bank account attached to the shell company. The resulting paper trail looks legitimate.

Zucman estimates that an amount equivalent to 8 percent of the world's household financial wealth is held, untaxed, in offshore accounts — around $8.6 trillion in 2016. "There's a great deal of opacity," he says. "You see all this wealth that belongs on paper, and authorities don't have a good way to pierce this veil of secrecy. They rely on the good will of bankers, which is not sufficient."

Accessing money in an offshore account is as easy as using a debit card from the offshore bank or taking out a loan in the United States against the assets held abroad. "You don't have to show up," Zucman says. "It can all be done remotely."

INSIDER TRADING

Employees at publicly held companies often possess something quite valuable to outside investors: knowledge about their employers' prospects beyond what has been issued in news releases. Those who would share — and perhaps illegally profit from — this intelligence in order to play the stock market know to circulate among their company's various departments, says Roomy Khan, a former analyst at Intel who went to prison for passing nonpublic information to Raj Rajaratnam, the billionaire founder and former chief of the Galleon Group hedge fund and others.

"I was always trying to make connections in the company's finance department and the marketing chain," Khan says. "In sales they know what the bookings are; in marketing they know what people are looking for." Because Intel controlled nearly 90 percent of the PC market for microchips when she was there, the intelligence gathering she did for Rajaratnam gave him the ability to predict the fortunes of Intel and the entire PC market.

When it comes to buying or selling stocks based on those predictions, insider traders must avoid being consistently accurate. Too many on-the-spot and out-of-the-ordinary trades that are correct can raise flags. "The government spots insider traders," says Khan, who now gives speeches to companies about the dangers of insider trading. The feds aren't the only ones monitoring unusual trades. Companies can get in trouble if they have too many leaks, and so can investment funds if they act on them, so both types of businesses are looking out for suspicious activity.

Social and professional circles can be used to draw out information from anyone willing to share secret details of products or strategies. "Let's say Samsung was having battery issues, and if my friend said something about the issues, I would start probing him. I know what the market is looking for," Khan says. "I would ask more and more detailed questions." Manipulation is the key to gaining confidential information, but insider traders try to be casual and friendly; people are more easily persuaded to share if they are made to feel powerful, wanted and included in the upper echelons of financial society. Khan says: "I used my lifestyle, my success, the trappings of success."

MONEY LAUNDERING

Illegal enterprises seek every possible way to get their cash back into circulation. To launder this dirty money in the United States requires them to "structure" their deposits of ill-gotten cash. Banks are required to report transactions involving $10,000 or more in cash, so their deposits need to be much smaller than that. "Criminals understand that U.S. banking laws have become a lot stricter in the last several years," says Adam Braverman, United States attorney for the Southern District of California. "They used to deposit $9,999 in 10 or 20 different banks. Now we look for those suspicious activities." Would-be launderers try to avoid triggering the software banks use to maintain anti-money-laundering controls by varying their deposits by amount, location — both geographically and institutionally — and even timing.

Prepaid debit cards like Green Dot offer more anonymous (and less labor-intensive) means of working dirty money into the system. "A new way organizations launder money is by purchasing gift cards or debit cards that they can resell and transfer money easily," Braverman says. Because anyone can buy such cards at a drugstore, for example, they're harder to trace than bank deposits, which require accounts. Purchasers still need to limit how much they put on debit cards to less than $10,000.

If launderers want to do things the old-fashioned way, they can smuggle cash across a border. It's best to vacuum-seal it or pack it with plastic wrap to reduce the bulk — a million dollars can take up a lot of space — and hire a courier to transport it in duffel bags to a country with lax banking laws. Once the money is in, say, a South American location where that's the case, dollars can be exchanged for the local currency at a casa de cambio.

The United Nations estimates that up to $1.6 trillion is laundered annually worldwide. Pop culture would have us believe that cash-driven businesses like strip clubs, car washes and casinos are the best places to clean up money. Dealing with the burden of running a legitimate business and paying actual taxes is anything but easy money.

Why Are American Prisons So Afraid of This Book?

BY JONAH ENGEL BROMWICH | JAN. 18, 2018

IN THE EIGHT YEARS since its publication, "The New Jim Crow," a book by Michelle Alexander that explores the phenomenon of mass incarceration, has sold well over a million copies, been compared to the work of W.E.B. Du Bois, been cited in the legal decisions to end stop-and-frisk and sentencing laws, and been quoted passionately on stage at the Academy Awards.

But for the more than 130,000 adults in prison in North Carolina and Florida, the book is strictly off-limits.

And prisoners around the country often have trouble obtaining copies of the book, which points to the vast racial disparities in sentencing policy, and the way that mass incarceration has ravaged the African-American population.

This month, after protests, New Jersey revoked a ban some of its prisons had placed on the book, while New York quickly scrapped a program that would have limited its inmates' ability to receive books at all.

Ms. Alexander, a civil rights lawyer and former clerk on the Supreme Court, said the barriers to reading the book are no accident.

"Some prison officials are determined to keep the people they lock in cages as ignorant as possible about the racial, social and political forces that have made the United States the most punitive nation on earth," she said. "Perhaps they worry the truth might actually set the captives free."

A spokeswoman for the Florida Department of Corrections confirmed that the book had been banned but would not elaborate. A form from the prison system's literature review committee obtained by The New York Times indicates that the book was rejected because it presented a security threat and was filled with what the document called "racial overtures."

Michelle Alexander in 2012. Her book on mass incarceration, "The New Jim Crow," has been banned by prisons in North Carolina and Florida.

In North Carolina prisons, "The New Jim Crow" has been banned multiple times, most recently on Feb. 24, 2017, when it was deemed "likely to provoke confrontation between racial groups." State policy dictates that such bans can last for only a year, so the book will be permitted in the state's prisons late next month — unless it is banned again.

"All you need is one prison to challenge it, and then the book goes back on the list," said Katya Roytburd, a volunteer with Prison Books Collective, a nonprofit that sends free books to prisoners in North Carolina and Alabama.

The central thesis of "The New Jim Crow" is that the mass incarceration of black people is an extension of the American tradition of racial discrimination.

It zeroes in on how the "law and order" rhetoric of the 1950s and 1960s led to the war on drugs and harsh law enforcement and sentencing policies, which disproportionately affect black people.

"It is no longer socially permissible to use race, explicitly, as a justification for discrimination, exclusion, and social contempt," she writes in the introduction. "So we don't. Rather than rely on race we use our criminal justice system to label people of color 'criminals' and then engage in all the practices we supposedly left behind."

Black people are still imprisoned at over five times the rate of white people, according to a 2016 report by The Sentencing Project, a prison reform advocacy group. And while a bipartisan push for sentencing reform took place during President Barack Obama's second term, those efforts have stalled under Attorney General Jeff Sessions and President Trump.

The choices prisons make when banning books can seem arbitrary, even capricious. In Texas, 10,000 titles are banned, including such head-scratchers as "The Color Purple" and a compilation by the humor writer Dave Barry.

"Mein Kampf," on the other hand, is permitted, along with several books by white nationalists, despite the existence of prison gangs like the murderous Aryan Brotherhood of Texas.

When you look at the banned book lists and specifically the stuff that's being allowed, there's a definite bias toward violent armed white supremacy and the censorship of anything that questions the existing religious or political status quo," said Paul Wright, the executive director of the Human Rights Defense Center.

Activists see bans as an indictment of how prisoners are limited more broadly. Amy Peterson, a member of NYC Books Through Bars, which sends books to inmates in 40 states, said books were often sent back with little explanation.

"It does seem very much up to the person in the shipping room who's making these arbitrary decisions," she said. "I see it as one of the many ways that people are deprived of basic rights in prison."

But for many incarcerated people, the ban on "The New Jim Crow" does not seem arbitrary. In 2014, Dominic Passmore, a prisoner in Michigan, ordered the book after checking to make sure that it had not been banned in the state. When it arrived, according to state documents, the prison's mailroom staff refused to give it to him, citing its racial content.

Months later, after a series of appeals, the state decided that Mr. Passmore could read the book but informed him that he would have to buy a new copy, as it had misplaced his.

Mr. Passmore, who spent nine years behind bars after pleading no contest to armed robbery charges when he was 14, eventually read the book. He said that it opened his eyes to the wrongs done to black people.

"I feel like the reason why they tried to reject it is because they didn't want me to have that kind of knowledge," said Mr. Passmore, who was recently released.

Prison officials almost universally agree that certain books should be prohibited. Roger Werholtz, who served as secretary of corrections in Kansas and as interim executive director of corrections in Colorado, said that books that could interfere with safety, like instructions on how to pick locks or make weapons, or those that could incite disturbances, such as racist or white supremacist literature, were banned under his watch.

He said that he did not think banning Ms. Alexander's book for its arguments about race made sense.

"I would be pretty skeptical of that," he said. "That's not anything that you don't see in the newspaper. Frankly, most prison officials talk very openly about the overrepresentation of minorities."

Jason Hernandez, 40, was a 21-year-old first-time, nonviolent drug offender when he was convicted of conspiracy to distribute crack cocaine. He was sentenced to life imprisonment without parole.

Mr. Hernandez studied law in prison and filed his own appeals, only to see them denied. In 2010, he borrowed "The New Jim Crow" from the prison's library lending program.

It inspired him to start a grass-roots organization to help himself and other nonviolent drug offenders with life sentences. In September

2011, he appealed directly to Mr. Obama for clemency. His request was granted and he was released in 2015.

"They prevent books from going in there that could maybe help people escape," he said. "This is what this book did for me, and what it's done for hundreds of others."

Harvey Weinstein 'Perp Walked' Into the Future of #MeToo

BY THE NEW YORK TIMES | MAY 25, 2018

This installment of the Gender Letter, a weekly take on news, trends and culture, is by Jessica Bennett, gender editor, and Maya Salam, a reporter for the Express Desk.

DEAR READERS,

They say a picture is worth a thousand words. In Harvey Weinstein's case, the image of the former film mogul in handcuffs on Friday, perp walking his way into the New York Police Department's First Precinct, in Lower Manhattan, two words may actually get the job done: Time's Up.

On Friday, Mr. Weinstein turned himself in on charges of rape and committing a criminal sex act for incidents involving two women. He walked in with a handful of books under his arm and emerged, an hour later, with three sets of handcuffs fastened to his wrists (they were linked in order to stretch across his back).

"He used to be the king of TriBeCa," tweeted Jodi Kantor, the New York Times reporter whose investigation with Megan Twohey broke the news of Mr. Weinstein's abuse. "Now he's turning himself in there."

Anyone who's been tasked with camping out at a police station, waiting for a criminal to be walked out, has seen this before. (Jessica's first job in journalism was the cops beat at The Boston Globe; Maya works on our breaking news team at The Times.)

But this perp walk by a man who once proclaimed himself untouchable, who claimed to have "eyes and ears everywhere," who represented a kind of male privilege and power that has long felt beyond reach — and who was led, restrained, into his arraignment by a female detective — felt as if it represented something larger.

Harvey Weinstein, center, turned himself in at the First Precinct in Lower Manhattan. He was charged with rape and committing a criminal sex act.

"We got you, Harvey Weinstein, we got you," tweeted the actress Rose McGowan, who was one of the first women to come forward publicly last fall about Mr. Weinstein's history of sexual misconduct. "I have to admit I didn't think I would see the day that he would have handcuffs on him," she said on ABC's "Good Morning America."

Asia Argento, an Italian actress and director who is among Mr. Weinstein's accusers, wrote on Twitter: "Today Harvey Weinstein will take his first step on his inevitable descent to hell. We, the women, finally have real hope for justice."

The perp walk is a long-debated practice in the criminal justice world. In France it is banned — in part because, as David Greenfield, a former city councilman from Brooklyn, once put it: "Even Mother Teresa dragged out by detectives would look guilty." (Mr. Greenfield proposed a local law in 2011 that would have banned the practice, but it was never put in place.)

But the sight of Mr. Weinstein in those handcuffs offered a tangible image, long-sought proof, that the collective sound of women's voices had been heard over the din.

Catharine A. MacKinnon, the trailblazing legal scholar who first defined sexual harassment, recently wrote that #MeToo had done what the law could not. The mass mobilization, she said, had eroded one of the biggest barriers to prosecuting sexual harassment: "the disbelief and trivializing dehumanization of its victims."

If women speaking out was the first phase of #MeToo, then the second is proving to be concrete legal ramifications — and public humiliation. Mr. Weinstein has lost the ability to go down quietly.

Below is a brief taxonomy of Mr. Weinstein's epic unraveling, as told through The New York Times's most notable coverage.

THE EXPOSÉ

A Pulitzer Prize-winning investigation by the reporters Jodi Kantor and Megan Twohey about the allegations against Mr. Weinstein, and about how he had for decades paid off his victims, opened the floodgates.

The article represented multiple women — among them the actresses Ashley Judd and Rose McGowan, who went on the record with specific allegations against the producer.

THE #METOO MOVEMENT TAKES SHAPE

New accusations of rape, groping and forced oral sex dating back to the 1970s began to pile up against Mr. Weinstein, as dozens of accusers continued to speak out, including the stars Gwyneth Paltrow and Angelina Jolie, who added their names to the #MeToo movement.

The personal accounts from women whose lives and careers were damaged by Mr. Weinstein's behavior left a deep mark on many Americans. Two of those women, the actresses Salma Hayek and Lupita Nyong'o, wrote about their chilling experiences with the mogul for our Opinion section.

THE UNRAVELING

First, Mr. Weinstein resigned from the Weinstein Company's board, which quickly descended into chaos. Hachette Book Group shut down the Weinstein Company's publishing imprint, Weinstein Books.

He was ousted from the Academy of Motion Picture Arts and Sciences, a rare action for the organization, which had awarded his studio five best picture Oscars, including for "Shakespeare in Love" and "The English Patient."

In March, the Weinstein Company filed for bankruptcy. This month, it named a Dallas private equity firm as the winning bidder in its bankruptcy sale, though plaintiffs suing the studio oppose the plan.

THE LEGAL CASE AGAINST HIM

On Friday, Mr. Weinstein was arrested and charged in New York. Prosecutors in Los Angeles and police in London have also been investigating sexual assault allegations against him. Federal prosecutors in Manhattan have broadened their inquiry into possible financial improprieties to include accusations that Mr. Weinstein violated federal stalking laws.

In 2015, the Manhattan district attorney, Cyrus R. Vance Jr., decided not to pursue sexual abuse charges after accusations by Ambra Battilana, a model from Italy, claiming that his office did not have enough evidence to prosecute.

WOMEN REACT TO HIS ARREST

The actresses Rose McGowan, Asia Argento, Mira Sorvino, Annabella Sciorra and others reacted to the news of Mr. Weinstein's arrest with satisfaction, relief and even joy.

Glossary

appurtenance An item that is associated with a style of living or a specific activity.

asseverate To claim or assert.

badinage Witty conversation.

cane bill-hook A tool used to cut sugar cane.

counterfeit An exact imitation of something valuable, often currency, with the intent to deceive.

Democrat Member of the Democratic Party, the first political party in the United States. Through the mid-20th century, the party had a conservative, pro-business stance.

emolument A fee, salary or profit from employment or holding a political office.

felony A serious crime, usually violent, that is most often punishable by more than a year in prison or sometimes by death.

graft The use of a politician's position of authority for personal gain.

grand larceny The theft of personal property that has a value above a legally specified amount.

indictment A formal accusation or charge of a crime.

policy-slip racket Illegal gambling in the form of a lottery played mostly by the poor or working class.

racial profiling The use of race, ethnicity or national origin to target individuals for suspicion of a crime.

red-light district An area of a city or town where sex businesses, such as brothels, are located.

Republican Member of the Republican Party, the forerunner of the modern Democratic Party that, in the 19th century, supported the abolition of slavery and the institution of civil rights for minorities.

scow trimmer A person who scavenged and recycled or sold waste materials transported on scows — flat-bottomed boats used to transport bulk materials and dredge channels.

speakeasy An illegal night club or liquor store that served alcohol during prohibition.

stuss A variation of the card game faro in which cards are dealt by hand and the house wins all bets when two equal cards are drawn; also called Jewish Faro.

Media Literacy Terms

"Media literacy" refers to the ability to access, understand, critically assess and create media. The following terms are important components of media literacy, and they will help you critically engage with the articles in this title.

angle The aspect of a news story on which a journalist focuses and develops.

attribution The method by which a source is identified or by which facts and information are assigned to the person who provided them.

balance Principle of journalism that both perspectives of an argument should be presented in a fair way.

chronological order Method of writing a story presenting the details of the story in the order in which they occurred.

commentary Type of story that is an expression of opinion on recent events by a journalist generally known as a commentator.

credibility The quality of being trustworthy and believable, said of a journalistic source.

critical review Type of story that describes an event or work of art, such as a theater performance, film, concert, book, restaurant, radio or television program, exhibition or musical piece, and offers critical assessment of its quality and reception.

editorial Article of opinion or interpretation.

feature story Article designed to entertain as well as to inform.

headline Type, usually 18 point or larger, used to introduce a story.

human interest story Type of story that focuses on individuals and how events or issues affect their lives, generally offering a sense of relatability to the reader.

impartiality Principle of journalism that a story should not reflect a journalist's bias and should contain balance.

intention The motive or reason behind something, such as the publication of a news story.

interview story Type of story in which the facts are gathered primarily by interviewing another person or persons.

motive The reason behind something, such as the publication of a news story or a source's perspective on an issue.

news story An article or style of expository writing that reports news, generally in a straightforward fashion and without editorial comment.

op-ed An opinion piece that reflects a prominent individual's opinion on a topic of interest.

paraphrase The summary of an individual's words, with attribution, rather than a direct quotation of their exact words.

quotation The use of an individual's exact words indicated by the use of quotation marks and proper attribution.

reliability The quality of being dependable and accurate, said of a journalistic source.

rhetorical device Technique in writing intending to persuade the reader or communicate a message from a certain perspective.

source The origin of the information reported in journalism.

style A distinctive use of language in writing or speech; also a news or publishing organization's rules for consistent use of language with regards to spelling, punctuation, typography and capitalization, usually regimented by a house style guide.

tone A manner of expression in writing or speech.

Media Literacy Questions

1. What type of story is "The White-Collar-Crime Cheat Sheet: How the Biggest Scammers Get Away With It" (on page 196)? Identify how the writer's tone and perspective help convey his opinion on the topic.

2. Do you find the article "Interesting from Kansas" (on page 13) to be credible? If so, in what ways? If not, why not?

3. Does the journalist demonstrate the principle of impartiality in the article "Gangsters Again Engaged in a Murderous War" (on page 49). If so, how? If not, how could they have made the article more impartial?

4. What is the intention of "Poverty and Crime." (on page 79)? How effectively does the writer achieve his intended purpose?

5. Identify the sources cited in the article "Citizens' Gun Use on Rise in Houston" (on page 132). How does the journalist attribute information to each of these sources in the article? How effective are the attributions in helping the reader identify them?

6. Compare the headlines of "The Confession of Constance Kent" (on page 32) and "23 More Undesirables Are Seized in Times Square as Round-Up Spreads" (on page 94). Which is a more compelling headline, and why? How could the less compelling headline be changed to better draw the reader's interest?

7. Is the article "The Ring Again; Another Batch of Indictments Against Tweed & Co." (on page 34) a commentary, news story or interview story? What elements of the article helped you draw your conclusion?

Citations

All citations in this list are formatted according to the Modern Language Association's (MLA) style guide.

BOOK CITATION

THE NEW YORK TIMES EDITORIAL STAFF. *Crime*. New York: New York Times Educational Publishing, 2019.

ONLINE ARTICLE CITATIONS

BORDERS, WILLIAM. "Narcotics Drive Raises Arrests ." *The New York Times*, 13 Oct. 1964, timesmachine.nytimes.com/timesmachine/1964/10/13/101496739.html.

BRADSHER, KEITH. "Daughter's Death Prompts Fight on 'Date Rape' Drug." *The New York Times*, 16 Oct. 1999, www.nytimes.com/1999/10/16/us/daughter -s-death-prompts-fight-on-date-rape-drug.html.

BROMWICH, JONAH ENGEL. "Why Are American Prisons So Afraid of This Book?" *The New York Times*, 18 Jan. 2018, www.nytimes.com/2018/01/18/us/new -jim-crow-book-ban-prison.html.

CALDWELL, EARL. "Negroes Held Oppressed by the Law." *The New York Times*, 1 Aug. 1971, www.nytimes.com/1971/08/01/archives/negroes-held -oppressed-by-the-law.html.

CHICAGO TRIBUNE. "Outrageous Rape." *The New York Times*, 21 Nov. 1856, timesmachine.nytimes.com/timesmachine/1856/11/21/101001545.html.

DIESENHOUSE, SUSAN. "A Rising Tide of Violence Leaves More Youths in Jail." *The New York Times*, 8 July 1990, www.nytimes.com/1990/07/08/weekinreview/the -nation-a-rising-tide-of-violence-leaves-more-youths-in-jail.html.

FRENKEL, SHEERA. "Ponzi Scheme Meets Ransomware for a Doubly Malicious Attack." *The New York Times*, 6 June 2017, www.nytimes.com/2017/06/06/ technology/hackers-ransomware-bitcoin-ponzi-wannacry.html.

GORDON, ALBERT J. "Crime Increasing in 'Little Spain.'" *The New York Times*, 3 Aug. 1947, timesmachine.nytimes.com/timesmachine/1947/08/03/99273574.html.

GRAHAM, FRED P. "Johnson Presses Anticrime Drive." *The New York Times*, 10 Mar. 1966, timesmachine.nytimes.com/timesmachine/1966/03/10/79970884.html.

GROSS, JANE. "A New, Purified Form of Cocaine Causes Alarm as Abuse Increases." *The New York Times*, 29 Nov. 1985, www.nytimes.com/1985/11/29/nyregion/a-new-purified-form-of-cocaine-causes-alarm-as-abuse-increases.html.

HOFFMAN, JAN. "Pregnant, Addicted — and Guilty?" *The New York Times*, 19 Aug. 1990, www.nytimes.com/1990/08/19/magazine/pregnant-addicted-and-guilty.html.

HOLMES, STEVEN A. "Senate Votes Sweeping Crime Bill, Banning Some Assault Weapons." *The New York Times*, 12 July 1990, www.nytimes.com/1990/07/12/us/senate-votes-sweeping-crime-bill-banning-some-assault-weapons.html.

JOHNSTON, DAVID. "U.S. Officials Lay Out Plan To Fight Computer Attacks." *The New York Times*, 17 Feb. 2000, www.nytimes.com/2000/02/17/business/us-officials-lay-out-plan-to-fight-computer-attacks.html.

LEWIS, NEIL A. "Law Professor Accuses Thomas Of Sexual Harassment in 1980s." *The New York Times*, 7 Oct. 1991, www.nytimes.com/1991/10/07/us/law-professor-accuses-thomas-of-sexual-harassment-in-1980-s.html.

LOWE, JAIME. "The White-Collar-Crime Cheat Sheet." *The New York Times*, 3 May 2018, www.nytimes.com/interactive/2018/05/03/magazine/money-issue-white-collar-crimes-cheat-sheet.html.

LUKAS, J. ANTHONY. "Police Battle Demonstrators in Street; Hundreds Injured." *The New York Times*, 29 Aug. 1968, timesmachine.nytimes.com/timesmachine/1968/08/29/90669084.html.

MALCOLM, ANDREW H. "Troubled Farmers: Debts and Guns." *The New York Times*, 12 Dec. 1985, www.nytimes.com/1985/12/12/us/troubled-farmers-debts-and-guns.html.

MARKHAM, JAMES M. "President Calls for 'Total War' on U.S. Addiction." *The New York Times*, 21 Mar. 1972, www.nytimes.com/1972/03/21/archives/president-calls-for-total-war-on-us-addiction-he-confers-in-city-on.html.

THE NEW-ORLEANS BEE. "A Negro Outbreak." *The New York Times*, 17 Aug. 1862, timesmachine.nytimes.com/timesmachine/1862/08/17/78695664.html.

THE NEW YORK TIMES. "Anti-Crime Body to Organize Today." *The New York Times*, 12 Aug. 1925, timesmachine.nytimes.com/timesmachine/1925/08/12/104181577.html.

THE NEW YORK TIMES. "Applicants Ruled by Politics." *The New York*

Times, 22 Dec. 1894, timesmachine.nytimes.com/timesmachine/1894/12/22/106845221.html.

THE NEW YORK TIMES. "Association Aids Crusade on Crime." *The New York Times*, 2 Aug. 1925, timesmachine.nytimes.com/timesmachine/1925/08/02/99351660.html.

THE NEW YORK TIMES. "Becker Wore Women's Clothes and Whiskers." *The New York Times*, 30 Aug. 1904, timesmachine.nytimes.com/timesmachine/1904/08/30/117947151.html.

THE NEW YORK TIMES. "Bootleggers Seize Agent as Hijacker." *The New York Times*, 9 Aug. 1924, timesmachine.nytimes.com/timesmachine/1924/08/09/104047188.html.

THE NEW YORK TIMES. "Burglary and Heavy Robbery in New London." *The New York Times*, 23 Sept. 1857, timesmachine.nytimes.com/timesmachine/1857/09/23/78506646.html.

THE NEW YORK TIMES. "Champagne Seized in Hoboken Dry Raid." *The New York Times*, 31 Dec. 1930, timesmachine.nytimes.com/timesmachine/1930/12/31/92133707.html.

THE NEW YORK TIMES. "Childhood and Crime." *The New York Times*, 29 Mar. 1860, timesmachine.nytimes.com/timesmachine/1860/03/29/91453861.html.

THE NEW YORK TIMES. "Citizens' Gun Use on Rise in Houston." *The New York Times*, 21 Nov. 1982, www.nytimes.com/1982/11/21/us/citizen-s-gun-use-on-rise-in-houston.html.

THE NEW YORK TIMES. "The Confession of Constance Kent." *The New York Times*, 12 Sept. 1865, timesmachine.nytimes.com/timesmachinc/1865/09/12/78750828.html.

THE NEW YORK TIMES. "Descent Upon 'Park Cruisers.' " *The New York Times*, 13 May 1857, timesmachine.nytimes.com/timesmachine/1857/05/13/78498382.html.

THE NEW YORK TIMES. "Fight Guns, Not Just Drugs." *The New York Times*, 8 Dec. 1990, www.nytimes.com/1990/12/08/opinion/fight-guns-not-just-drugs.html.

THE NEW YORK TIMES. "Final Action at Capital; Proclaims the End of Prohibition Law." *The New York Times*, 6 Dec. 1933, timesmachine.nytimes.com/timesmachine/1933/12/06/105826298.html.

THE NEW YORK TIMES. "Gangsters Again Engaged in a Murderous War." *The New York Times*, 9 June 1912, timesmachine.nytimes.com/timesmachine/1912/06/09/100369688.html.

THE NEW YORK TIMES. "Hardships Suffered by Unionists." *The New York Times*, 26 Jan. 1862, timesmachine.nytimes.com/timesmachine/1862/01/26/

78676753.html.

THE NEW YORK TIMES. "Harvey Weinstein 'Perp Walked' Into the Future of #MeToo." *The New York Times*, 25 May 2018, www.nytimes.com/2018/05/25/us/harvey-weinstein-perp-walk.html.

THE NEW YORK TIMES. "Heavy Sentences for Murder, Manslaughter and Assault." *The New York Times*, 9 May 1859, timesmachine.nytimes.com/timesmachine/1859/05/09/78891560.html.

THE NEW YORK TIMES. " 'Hot Summer'; Race Riots in North." *The New York Times*, 26 July 1964, www.nytimes.com/1964/07/26/archives/hot-summer-race-riots-in-north.html.

THE NEW YORK TIMES. "Interesting from Kansas." *The New York Times*, 22 Nov. 1856, timesmachine.nytimes.com/timesmachine/1856/11/22/77064810.html.

THE NEW YORK TIMES. "Law Courts; Court of General Sessions." *The New York Times*, 13 Oct. 1853, timesmachine.nytimes.com/timesmachine/1853/10/13/87871212.html.

THE NEW YORK TIMES. "Liquor Still Flows into Boston." *The New York Times*, 9 May 1925, timesmachine.nytimes.com/timesmachine/1925/05/09/101663839.html.

THE NEW YORK TIMES. "Militants Vow to Continue Protest at Harlem Church." *The New York Times*, 4 Jan. 1970, timesmachine.nytimes.com/timesmachine/1970/01/04/354671172.html.

THE NEW YORK TIMES. "Poverty and Crime." *The New York Times*, 23 Aug. 1925, timesmachine.nytimes.com/timesmachine/1925/08/23/119052458.html.

THE NEW YORK TIMES. "Prison Population Seen Up After War." *The New York Times*, 21 Nov. 1943, timesmachine.nytimes.com/timesmachine/1943/11/21/83952383.html.

THE NEW YORK TIMES. "Prominent Trader Accused of Defrauding Clients." *The New York Times*, 11 Dec. 2008, dealbook.nytimes.com/2008/12/11/prominent-trader-accused-of-defrauding-clients/.

THE NEW YORK TIMES. "Quintet Raids Drake Hotel." *The New York Times*, 30 July 1925, timesmachine.nytimes.com/timesmachine/1925/07/30/98836323.html.

THE NEW YORK TIMES. "A Remedy for Many Ills; The Great Demand for Cocaine Springing Up." *The New York Times*, 2 Sept. 1885, timesmachine.nytimes.com/timesmachine/1885/09/02/109782754.html.

THE NEW YORK TIMES. "The Ring Again; Another Batch of Indictments Against

Tweed & Co." *The New York Times*, 10 Mar. 1871, timesmachine
.nytimes.com/timesmachine/1871/03/10/80312413.html.

THE NEW YORK TIMES. "30 Taken in Bronx Raid." *The New York Times*, 4 Jan.
1930, timesmachine.nytimes.com/timesmachine/1930/01/04/94227563.html.

THE NEW YORK TIMES. "23 More Undesirables Are Seized in Times Square as
Round-Up Spreads." *The New York Times*, 1 Aug. 1954, timesmachine.nytimes
.com/timesmachine/1954/08/01/92831866.html.

THE NEW YORK TIMES. "Warring on Crime." *The New York Times*, 16 Feb. 1965,
timesmachine.nytimes.com/timesmachine/1965/02/16/101527628.html.

STAPLES, BRENT. "Why Some Get Busted — and Some Go Free." *The New York
Times*, 10 May 1999, https://www.nytimes.com/1999/05/10/opinion/
editorial-observer-why-some-get-busted-and-some-go-free.html.

WALDRON, MARTIN. "Violent Crimes Up in Jersey Suburbs." *The New York
Times*, 4 Nov. 1979, www.nytimes.com/1979/11/04/archives/violent-crimes
-up-in-jersey-suburbs-vandalism-by-teenagers-a-major.html.

WEST, DEBRA. "Aftermath of Internet Pedophilia Case: Guilt, and a New
Awareness of Danger." *The New York Times*, 12 July 2000, www.nytimes.com/
2000/07/12/nyregion/aftermath-of-internet-pedophilia-case-guilt-and-a-new
-awareness-of-danger.html.

Index